Acclaim *for* the authors of HOLIDAY WISHES

KA

“A
fu

“Fi
un
thi

ST
“A
he
ma

“D
his
wa

MA
“Th
me

“Pu a
partw
—*Ro*

Kate Austin has worked as a legal assistant, a commercial fisher, a brewery manager, a teacher, a technical writer and a herring popper. She lives in Vancouver, Canada, and would be delighted to hear from readers through her Web site, www.kateaustin.ca.

Stevi Mittman likes telling people she's left historical romance to write hysterical mysteries. *Who Needs June in December, Anyway?* is her third story for Harlequin NEXT in her LIFE ON LONG ISLAND CAN BE MURDER series featuring Teddi Bayer. In addition to the books, Stevi is blogging on her Web site (www.stevimittman.com), while Teddi blogs on her own interior design site (www.TipsFromTeddi.com).

Mary Schramski holds a Ph.D. in creative writing and enjoys teaching and encouraging other writers. She lives in Nevada with her husband—her daughter lives close by. Visit Mary's Web site at www.maryschramski.com.

Holiday Wishes

Kate Austin
Stevi Mittman
Mary Schramski

HOLIDAY WISHES

isbn-13:978-0-373-88120-8

isbn-10: 0-373-88120-7

This edition published by arrangement with Harlequin Books S.A.

TheNextNovel.com

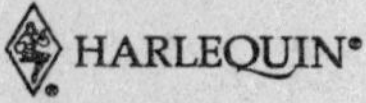

PRINTED IN U.S.A.

CONTENTS

IF I MAKE IT THROUGH DECEMBER

KATE AUSTIN

To Stevi and Mary. Thanks, it was great fun.

CHAPTER 1

You know how there's good luck and bad luck? And then there's the bad luck that gets all gussied up in fancy clothes and expensive shoes pretending it's good luck?

That's the kind of luck that came knocking on my door on a rainy and cold November day.

"Heather James?" the man at my office door asked.

I examined him carefully before I answered. He was in his fifties, I guessed, but his solemnity of manner made him appear older. Much older. He wore a black suit that fitted like it had been made for him—it probably had been—a subdued silk tie—definitely not the two for twenty dollar kind—and a blindingly white shirt, with initials on the cuffs.

I could see how he'd made it past the receptionist without fuss or announcement.

"Yes?" I answered, standing from behind my desk, kept spotlessly clean for just these events. Not that this kind of event had ever happened before. In over twenty years, no client had ever come to my office. I didn't do clients, I did paper. And calculations. The occasional e-mail and even fewer telephone calls.

"Ms. James," he said, holding out his tanned hand, shooting his wrist from beneath the starched cuff, the wrist embellished with a discreet but obviously real gold watch.

My impression of him, already at the top end of our client scale, moved upward. His portfolio, his tax planning, had to be one of our largest.

So why was he in *my* office?

It was immutable practice for clients to be seen in the office of our senior partner. Four or five times the size of mine, it contained leather furniture, mahogany tables, *real* art—I glanced over at my poster of Canaletto's *View of the Ducal Palace in Venice*—and an executive washroom which I snuck in to use, always before the cleaning staff had arrived to clean it, on the many late nights when I was the only one in the office.

I shook his bone-dry and polished hand and waited.

"You are Heather James?"

I nodded.

"Might I see some identification?"

I frowned, but remembering the stories I'd heard from my associates about some of our clients, I complied, handing him my driver's license without looking at it myself. I knew I looked like a troll under a bridge, my hair flattened on my head, my face pasty and my eyes lost in my head. I never looked at my license. Or the photo on my passport. Partly because the photographs were hideous and partly because I didn't want the reminder of how old I was.

How old? Forty-five. Still single. Still saving for that retirement fund in lieu of dating.

He perused my license, handed it back to me and nodded. "Your mother's name?"

This was beginning to feel like a call from my credit card company. But I'd neither lost nor overused my credit card—I never carried a balance, I'm a tax planner for God's sake. It was zero. As always. Paying interest on credit cards was a complete waste of money, money that could more properly reside in my retirement fund.

I answered anyway, "Donna. Donna Luongi," using her maiden name because I'd somehow gotten into the credit card company mode.

"Do you have proof of that?"

Weirder and weirder. But I'd bought into the first weirdness and now my curiosity—usually well under control—was out of it. Control, that is.

I turned to the locked fireproof filing cabinet beside my desk and pulled out my personal file.

"My birth certificate," I said with a flourish. "See." I pointed to my mother's name. "Right there."

"Ms. James, did you ever meet your Great-Aunt Francesca?"

I didn't know I had a Great-Aunt Francesca.

"She was your grandmother's baby sister."

I didn't know my grandmother. Or any other of my mother's relatives, for that matter. They were all dead before

I was born, or at least that's what my mother told me. Their deaths were followed by my parents' when I was twenty.

I nodded and waited for the next revelation. This conversation had definitely moved out of the credit call pattern and into the unknown great-aunt dying and leaving me a fortune pattern.

"Francesca died almost six months ago," he continued. "It took some time to find you." The accusation in his voice was clear. Obviously, I should have kept in touch with Great-Aunt Francesca even though I hadn't known she existed.

"You are her only living relative and her heir."

"Oh," I said, flabbergasted by this confirmation of the pattern.

Now, of course, he would tell me I'd inherited some decrepit old house in the middle of nowhere where I'd have to spend a year before it became mine to sell. I'd seen this movie before.

I contemplated the size of my retirement fund and grinned. The inheritance meant nothing to me except headaches.

"Do you know Francesca's Ristorante downtown?"

Not at all the question I'd been expecting.

"I was there once," I replied. "Too noisy for me."

What I meant was that it was too Italian, too exuberant, too, well, too much of everything. Food and noise and music and people. Too much wine. Too much color. Too much excitement.

Not the kind of place Heather James, who spent her days and nights engrossed in spreadsheets, would go to more than once.

"You're the new owner."

CHAPTER 2

I did all the things a prudent accountant and tax planner should do. I got a copy of the will from Mr. Simon. I asked for and had delivered to me Francesca's accounting and personnel files.

She had very well organized files and I tried not to wonder whether I'd inherited my passion for order from her. It certainly hadn't come from either of my parents. They had died in debt and with their papers in such a mess it had taken me months to make sense of them and another year to bring everything up to date.

I checked the lease, the taxes, the zoning. I did bylaw searches and corporate searches. I met with Francesca's one-day-a-week bookkeeper.

It took me seven days, but at the end of it I was confident that I knew the appropriate asking price for the restaurant—whether I decided to sell it as an ongoing business or for its assets. And I was confident that I'd get it and that I'd have the money before the end of the year. Perfect for tax planning.

Now all I had to do was make a visual inspection and I could list it. I always did an inspection of my projects. Over the years, that inspection had saved my clients a lot of money and me a boatload of aggravation. One dinner two years ago was not a sufficient inspection.

I took Monday as a vacation day. Francesca's keys were in my pocket and I knew the restaurant didn't open until noon. I set my alarm for five-thirty and figured on three or even four hours before anyone might show up.

I'd do my inspection and be out of there before anyone even knew I'd been.

The restaurant looked a bit worn in the gloomy predawn almost-light. Without the neon sign, dusty curtains drawn, it appeared tawdry and sad. I tried to remember how it had been two years earlier but could bring forward only an impression of light and color and noise.

Obviously, Francesca had let the place go over the past couple of years. That's what happened when you got old and kept working and that's why my retirement plan was so important. I didn't intend to be working past my prime. It was embarrassing. I'd rather be holed up in my paid-for condo in some sunny place in the south with other people just like me.

I reluctantly revised my asking price downwards. I knew that a quick sale depended on the right price. No one in their right mind would pay top dollar for a place like this. No matter how good the numbers might appear.

I patted myself on the back for doing the on-site inspection as I put my key in the lock. It would save me a lot of grief. I only hoped there were no more nasty surprises inside.

There were.

One at least. A man in white—no, not a ghost, I told myself—shot out of a chair at the front desk.

"Who the hell are you? And what are you doing in *my* restaurant?"

"*Your* restaurant?" I screamed back, channeling my mother for the first time in my grown-up life.

Heather James did not scream. I took a deep breath and tried again.

"Who are you?" Modulating my tone from a scream to a loud but calm yell.

"I," he said, pounding his chest, "am Sam Cappelletti and this is my restaurant."

He waved his arms around like a conductor, encompassing every inch of the dim and dusty room. The chairs, the tables, the linen, the unlit lights and the silverware.

"This beautiful place is mine. I—" pounding his chest again "—I am the chef."

"Then it's *not* your restaurant, is it? You're just the cook. I..." I yelled, taking a page from his book and pounding my chest, "am the new owner. This is *my* restaurant."

Suddenly, the ape man turned to a lover. He threw his arms around me, hugging so hard I was certain I heard my ribs crack.

"You're the new owner? Francesca's family?"

His voice, low and sexy with a faint accent—Italian, of course—tickled in my ear. I didn't care if it felt good, Sam Cappelletti was a long way out of line. I pulled away, drew myself to my full five feet ten inches, and smiled when I realized I was at least an inch taller than him. I poked him in the chest.

"Back off," I yelled, not even trying to stop myself this time.

I blamed the noise on the restaurant; you couldn't help but yell in this noisy place. I ignored the fact that except for my loud voice there wasn't a sound in it. The memory made me do it.

"Yes, I'm the new owner. But not for long."

I waved the listing agreement at him.

"I just have to sign this and Francesca's Ristorante is as good as sold. Now," I said, briskly, "let's turn the lights on and you can give me a tour."

The look on Sam Cappelletti's face could have curdled milk. It stopped my forward momentum dead. A combination of rage and a sorrow so strong he might have lost a parent or a child. I sympathized with that grief, softening for a moment, then chose to ignore it.

I examined him for the first time, looking past the chef whites. He wasn't tall, but the body beneath his clothes was strong—I'd felt the strength when he hugged me. Tanned olive skin matched his dark eyes and curly black hair.

He interrupted my examination with one of his own, nowhere near as admiring. His eyes dismissed my navy suit, white shirt and low-heeled pumps. He sniffed at my short, neat haircut and minimal makeup.

"You," he said, disdain evident in his voice, "have no idea about this restaurant. You are only an accountant."

He said the word as if it were an insult, the same way I'd used the word *cook* earlier. But it didn't matter what he said or how he said it.

"I don't think it matters what I am," I said, drawing my dignity carefully around me. "All you have to remember is that I'm the owner. And your employer."

He shrugged and turned away.

"Not so fast, Mr. Cappelletti. Since you're here—and why are you here so early?"

Visions of robbery or drug dealing ran through my head. Why was he in a restaurant that didn't open until noon? At six o'clock in the morning?

"I'm always here this early. I come in to work out the menu for the day, what we need to order, and then I go to the market."

"Every day?" He worked as hard as I did. "You get paid overtime every day?"

I knew exactly how much he made and it was substantially more than me.

"Sorry," I said. "Of course you don't. So why?"

"The reason Francesca's is such a success is because of our food. Good *fresh* food."

Well, that good fresh food was going to get paid for by someone else soon enough. I started walking, no longer waiting for Sam Cappelletti to start me on my tour.

Actually, I thought, inspecting the tables and linens, Sam Cappelletti trailing along behind me, maybe it was in better shape than it had appeared to be from the street.

I opened the floor-to-ceiling mahogany wine cellar with the key marked for it. I couldn't help but gasp at the hundreds of bottles lined up in a tower that reached far over my head. Even wine stores didn't have this much wine in stock.

"Why?" I couldn't finish my question, but the man who'd been silently ghosting along behind me answered anyway.

"On a busy Saturday night we might sell two hundred bottles of wine. All different kinds and prices. There are extra cases of our most popular wines in the basement."

"This is a lot of money tied up in inventory."

The rest of the tour went downhill from there. Sam didn't let me out of his sight nor did he answer any more of my questions. That was fine by me—I'd planned to make this inspection alone.

An hour later, he finally spoke. "You won't sell Francesca's now," he said. "Not before the holidays."

"Sure I will. It's attractively priced and everything looks good."

I made a note to myself to make sure that potential buyers saw the restaurant for the first time at night. The place looked okay now but much better with the lights and music on and customers in the seats. I resigned myself to a week of dinners at Francesca's, showing purchasers its charms.

"No restaurants sell in November or December. Everyone waits to buy until January. Numbers are down and they think they'll get a better deal."

Sam turned out to be right.

CHAPTER 3

Three days after the inspection I was forced—against my far better judgment—to admit that Sam Cappelletti had been correct. I'd spoken to half a dozen real estate agents who specialized in restaurants and they were certain that there was no way I'd be able to sell Francesca's now, and not likely in January or February, either. March seemed to be the consensus of opinion.

"You have to make sure you look after your asset until then if you want top dollar for it."

I believed in taking the advice of professionals but I also believed in second opinions. And third and fourth ones. I was aiming for the fifth opinion when it hit me.

Hire a manager.

But hiring a top-notch manager in November—and I wasn't about to settle for anything less—seemed to be about as likely as selling the damned restaurant in time to get my tax break.

I was stubborn but I wasn't stupid.

A week later I took two months of vacation time—only

a third of what they owed me—and became the new manager of Francesca's Ristorante.

Day One—Monday.

Closed.

Things went pretty well.

I arrived at seven o'clock. No one—and by that I meant Sam Cappelletti, the only member of my staff I'd met—was there. I headed directly for Francesca's office and spent the morning transferring back all the files I'd had delivered to me.

The morning felt just like a regular day, me in my office playing with numbers.

Day Two—Tuesday

Things weren't quite so simple.

I arrived at seven o'clock to find Sam waiting for me.

"Come on," he said, grabbing my hand and his coat from the chair, "we're going to the market."

"Not me," I insisted, pulling away. "That's not my job."

"Yes, you. And it is your job. Would you ever try to sell a project to your clients that you didn't know every single detail about? Would you ever recommend an investment you hadn't researched to death?"

He had me there. I wouldn't. And even if I was going to sell Francesca's the minute it was viable—even if I didn't feel at all like an owner of a restaurant but only a caretaker—Sam Cappelletti was right.

Of course I wouldn't say that out loud, but I did let him lead me out of the office to the parking lot where he helped me into a nondescript white van.

Somehow, it wasn't at all the car I had expected my chef to be driving. An Italian sports car—Lamborghini, Maserati, even a Fiat—but a boring ten-year-old white van? No way. Yet he drove that van as if it were a sports car, swerving in and out of traffic like a Formula 1 driver.

I put on my sunglasses—didn't matter that it was still dark, the less I could see of the traffic, the near misses, the silently screaming motorists, the better—and tightened my seat belt until I could barely breathe. I clung to the dashboard in front of me and whispered under my breath.

"It's only fifteen minutes. It's only fifteen minutes away."

I couldn't pull my hands from the dashboard to look at my watch so I counted seconds. The brakes squealed when I hit eleven hundred seconds and I carefully removed my cramped hands from the dashboard.

Sam laughed as I swung to face him.

"You idiot," I screamed. "You could have killed us."

"But I didn't, did I? Come along, Ms. Owner. I've got something to show you."

He took my hand—again—and walked me from the still dark parking lot into the market. Transfixed, I stopped dead in my tracks while early shoppers bustled around me and I ignored the bumps and hisses as they hurried past.

I felt as if I'd been parachuted into another world, a world I hadn't realized existed in my city. The space glowed.

Piles of fruit towered over me, reds and greens and golds, each piece placed with care and exactitude. The stalls were works of art—each one with its own special twist on the pile.

Some built up from a flat base, twenty Granny Smith apples by twenty Granny Smith apples wide, each layer containing a few less apples, until at the top, a single perfect green apple waited for the exacting customer to pick it.

The next stall over had figured out a way to pile their apples—shiny red Macs this time—in circles. I wondered if the bottom layer was pinned to the table so they wouldn't move out of alignment.

The next stall had the apples—I had to read the handwritten sign to figure out what kind they were—piled all higgledy-piggledy. They were Ambrosias, soft yellows and pinks and a tiny hint of red all mixed in together. And I couldn't resist.

The fruit called to me, "Pick me, pick me." And I did, putting half a dozen apples in a crinkly brown paper bag and handing them to the smiling woman behind the counter.

"Take this one," she said, holding out what appeared to be the most perfect apple in the universe, the apple the

Wicked Queen handed Snow White. I ignored the fairy tale and took the apple.

The punch of sweet crunchiness almost dropped me to the floor. I'd never eaten an apple like this one.

"Good?" Sam Cappelletti asked as he herded me away from the fruit stands and deeper into the market.

"Hmmmm." I nodded, taking another bite of the apple. "You want one?"

He shook his head and leaned in toward me. "Just a bite of yours," he said, waiting.

I looked down at my apple and across at him. Why not? What could it hurt? His teeth were sharp and white and the color of his lips matched the red on my apple. I shivered and pulled away again.

We raced through the part of the market that made bread, my mouth watering at the smell of it. Rich and warm and yeasty—I wanted to try it all.

By this time, the gloomy November day and the frightening drive over might never have been. I was hooked. And that was before we made it to the vegetable section.

There were vegetables I'd never seen before, never even imagined. I lingered at the smallest stall, a single wooden table filled with peppers, from the tiniest pepper ever grown to the head-of-cabbage-sized bell peppers.

"Don't touch that." Sam's voice came from behind me. "You'll be sorry."

I ignored him and brought the tiny green pepper to my

nose. It had no aroma and its skin was as soft as a kitten. I rubbed it against my cheek, my nose, my lips.

Sam laughed. "You'll see," he said. "Come on, we're out of here."

CHAPTER 4

I'd thought that the ride to the market was as bad as the day could get. I was wrong.

I didn't even notice whether the ride back to Francesca's was as hair-raising as the trip to the market.

"What's wrong with me?"

I sat in the front seat of the van, the visor down in front of me, and stared at my face in the pockmarked mirror. Red blotches had appeared on my cheeks and my lips were swollen to twice their normal size. My nose looked like I should be guiding a dozen reindeer through the foggy Christmas night.

"I told you not to touch that pepper. It's the hottest one in the world. I use two pairs of gloves when I work with it."

I put my face in my hands and moaned. "You should have stopped me," I said. "Why'd you let me do it?"

"You're the boss." He grinned. "And I did warn you. *You* didn't listen."

"It'll go away, won't it? I won't look like this forever."

"Just a couple of days," Sam said. "You should have listened to me."

I heard his snicker underneath the words.

"I could fire you, you know."

"You could, but you won't. How else are you going to get through December? It's our busiest month of the year, every restaurant's busiest month, and you'd never find another chef."

He grinned at me, his glee plain.

"Do you know how to cook for a hundred and twenty people every night? All of whom want something different and at different times?"

I shook my head.

"I thought not. You won't fire me."

He was right. I wouldn't fire him. But the next five minutes flew by as I imagined the scene. Me firing Sam Cappelletti. I set the scene in Francesca's office, me behind the desk, Sam standing crestfallen in front of it.

He'd beg for his job back and I'd ignore him. I'd tell him that I didn't need him, I'd found a much better chef than him, a woman, I'd gloat. One who could cook better than Sam Cappelletti had ever dreamed of.

Of course I couldn't fire him. But I saved the scene in my memory bank for the next time—surely not too far in the future—when he aggravated me again.

The drive back to the restaurant seemed to take an hour and by the time we arrived at Francesca's my burning face reminded me of the winter I'd gone to Mexico and forgotten that I hadn't been in the sun in five years.

That year my entire body had felt like it was on fire. It had been the vacation from hell, even if I ignored the sunstroke or the hives from the not-quite-ripe strawberries in my margaritas.

"Come with me, Ms. Owner," Sam said. "I'll fix your face for you."

And there it was—five minutes later and I already needed to retrieve the firing scene from my memory bank. I took a few minutes to contemplate the possibility of being an absentee owner and discarded it. I'd spend way too much time worrying about what was happening at the restaurant. I'd spend way too much time worrying about Sam Cappelletti.

No, I had to stay on.

So I met my staff for the first time wearing a thin coat of tea leaves soaked in baking soda on my face. At least it meant I wasn't scratching or crying when I met them.

Sam, laughing his fool head off, ushered each staff member into the chair in front of the desk in Francesca's office as they arrived, starting with the kitchen staff, moving on to the waiters and busboys—they were all male at Francesca's—and ending up with the bartender and the hostess.

I tried to smile without cracking the tea leaf paste but, from the looks on the faces of the people in front of me, the smile left something to be desired.

I met three dishwashers and part-time choppers—Sam called them choppers and I had a feeling that it was somehow more dignified than calling them dishwashers, though I had no idea why that might be—and after the first one I even remembered to write down their names.

Joey, Brown Bill and Red Bill. Each of them looked as if they'd just rolled out of bed and hadn't managed either a shower or a cup of coffee. I sent them off to the kitchen with a wave and an order to have a cup of coffee before they picked up any sharp objects.

Two assistants. Definitely snootier than the dishwashers, these women wore chefs' whites and checked pants and still managed to look as if they'd been dressed by Chanel. I wondered if Sam hired them—he'd already informed me that *he* hired everyone who worked in the kitchen—for their looks.

Linda and Delores. One blonde, one redhead. One French and one Russian. I chose not to think about their immigration status.

Waiters numbered eight. All ages from thirty to sixty. Dressed in white shirts, dark pants and silk ties. Daryl, James, Alberto, Jack, Silvio, Terry, Brad, Mario. I knew I wouldn't be able to tell them apart, maybe not ever.

Finally the bartender and the hostess arrived hand in hand. And it was more than obvious what they'd been doing this morning. Mark and Melissa.

He was short, chubby and looked and sounded like Bob Hoskins. She was tall and slim and looked as if a strong wind would knock her over.

Sixteen. I had sixteen people—including Sam Cappelletti—to worry about and that was just at lunch. Add in the cleaners who came in the middle of the night, the part-time bookkeeper who I was going to let go any minute, and my total staff numbered twenty.

And not one of them, except Sam, had laughed when they saw my face. I gave them bonus marks for that diplomacy.

Now I just had to figure out what they all did. And what I was supposed to do with them.

CHAPTER 5

My first day on the job and there was absolutely no way in hell I could walk through the restaurant. Any customer who saw me would vomit and Sam would take that as an excuse to remind me of how much I *didn't* know about running a restaurant.

He was right. I had absolutely no idea what I was doing but I was going to do it anyway. As soon as I could appear in public, I was going to do what all the business books told me I had to do.

I was going to shadow each and every employee in the restaurant to learn their job from the ground up. I'd start with the choppers and move up, right on through the waiters and bartender and hostess. I'd save Sam Cappelletti for last. Hopefully, by the time I got to the end of my list, I'd be really, really good at it.

Meanwhile, trapped in my office like the Man in the Iron Mask in his dungeon, I surfed the Internet for answers.

How long would my face burn?

Somewhere between twenty-four and seventy-two hours.

Did I need to go to the hospital?

Only if I got the capsicum in my eyes and didn't wash it out in time.

I locked my hands in my lap.

Why do my hands burn even though I've washed them at least a dozen times?

It takes time to get rid of the pain. Don't wash your hands too much or you'll add another type of stress to your already stressed nerves.

Don't touch your eyes. Don't touch your face. Don't touch any delicate part of your body. At the thought of the one untouched delicate part of my body, I cringed.

I stopped drinking from the bottle of water I'd brought with me and resolved to wrap my hands in tissue the next time I headed for the washroom.

"Heather?" A timid knock on the office door accompanied the quiet voice saying my name.

"Yes?"

"Can I come in?"

The etiquette for entering offices was obviously different here at Francesca's than it was in my real office. Anyone who'd heard my Yes? would already be in the door and sitting down at the chair opposite my desk without waiting for permission.

"Come on in," I said, pulling the tea leaves from my face and adding another layer of damp baking soda to the skin.

The mirror on my desk reflected back a thin layer of

white, completely unable to hide the blazing red face beneath it.

"Ouch," the hostess said, looking at my face. "You have to be careful in those tanning salons. I burnt my nipples the very first time I went there. I don't go anymore."

She didn't have to tell me that. Her skin was almost as white as the baking soda on my face, but she looked healthy. *Just a little too thin*, whispered the Rubenesque babe sitting in my chair.

"I've forgotten your name," I said. "Sit down."

"Melissa. I'm the hostess."

"Hmm. I remember your job, just didn't remember your name. I've had a rough day."

"You went to the tanning salon this morning?"

"It wasn't a tanning salon. It was a pepper. Green. Tiny." I held out the thumb and index finger of my right hand. "About this big." I estimated an inch with my fingers. "Big punch for a little pecker."

Melissa giggled. "Yeah, I've met a few of those myself."

"What can I do for you?"

"Nothing for me. I thought I'd drop in before the evening rush and see if you wanted anything. You didn't eat lunch. I can get you something from the kitchen, or if you want, I'll run across the street and pick you up a burger.

"Sam won't cook burgers. He says they ruin his grill so if any of us want one, we go across the street to Joe's. He makes good burgers."

"Sam doesn't mind?"

"Nope. Although most of us eat here most of the time. It's cheaper. And easier. By the time lunch is over, all I want to do is sit down and put up my feet. Get ready for the early drinkers. Even crossing the street to Joe's is too far."

"You don't go home in the afternoon?"

"Sometimes."

And I knew exactly what days Melissa managed to get home in the afternoon. When Mark could go home with her.

"We don't live that far from here."

Had I said it out loud? Or was Melissa reading my mind? Didn't matter, she knew I knew and didn't care a bit.

"I don't think I could eat a thing," I said. "But thanks for offering."

"No problem. Just let me know if there's anything I can do." She gestured at my face. "I've got some sleeping pills if you think you might need them."

Melissa stalked out of the office in her little black skirt and tall black heels. Nice, I thought, much nicer than she appeared at first glance.

The door swung open and Sam appeared carrying a tray.

"You don't knock?"

"Please. How would I knock carrying this? Come on, Ms. Owner, you need to eat something."

"I can't."

"Yes, you can. The food will make you feel better and it'll

help the swelling and burning go away. Everything I've made is very soft, very bland. It'll help. I promise."

While he was talking, he'd been working at the table in the corner. He started with a pale pink tablecloth, added a vase of white orchids with pink throats, two plates, cutlery, glasses and a silver pitcher shimmering with water droplets. A bowl of pasta, a green salad, a loaf of lightly browned bread completed the picture.

He placed two silver candlesticks on the table and lit the candles, then closed the door and turned out the lights in the office.

"There," he said. "Now it's time for you to eat. It'll be a long night if you're staying until closing and you'll never make it without having something to eat."

He was right. Again. As much as I hated to admit it, Sam Cappelletti knew at least a thousand times more about the restaurant business than I did. It wouldn't hurt me to take advantage of his knowledge.

"Thanks," I said. "I don't know how much I can eat, but I'll try."

"Good."

The pasta, each piece curled around itself like a pig's tail, smelled like butter, cheese and the faintest touch of earth.

"What's that smell? It's like dirt. Good, clean dirt."

"Escargot," Sam said. "Not a lot, just enough for flavor. Try it," he continued, placing a spoonful on my plate. "I guarantee you'll like it."

Guarantee notwithstanding, I wasn't about to put anything containing snails in my mouth. I could feel the tea leaves cracking on my scrunched up face.

"Don't look at me like that. You'll like it. Really."

"No snails." I put my hand over my mouth, denying any earth creatures access. "No snails. No truffles. No worms."

"No worms. I never cook with worms. Eels, occasionally. Escargot quite a bit. Truffles as much as I can. Never worms."

He lifted a fork to my lips.

"Come on, Ms. Owner. You can't own a restaurant where you can't eat the food. What if some high roller customer asks you to sit down and try what he's eating? You can't look at him as if he's crazy. You just have to try it."

"Maybe," I said, "but that doesn't mean I have to eat snails in my own office." I slapped the table for emphasis.

Sam waggled the fork in front of me. "One bite, okay? You can spit it out if you don't like it."

One bite and I was hooked. I ate the entire bowl of pasta, the salad and the half loaf of Italian bread that had come with it.

"Okay," I said, "you're right. It was delicious. But I still don't want to eat snails, not whole ones, anyway."

He smiled at me and left the office.

One of the busboys—Brown Bill, I think—hurried in after him and cleaned up the table without saying a word.

CHAPTER 6

I sat in my office and tried to decipher the aromas wafting in from the restaurant. I heard the clink of wine bottles and glasses, the Puccini, a little too loud for my taste, blaring from the speakers and the laughter of my customers.

I read the menu and the wine list Melissa had brought me during the afternoon lull, saying, "Sam thinks you should read this."

I weighed the wine list in my hand. I knew nothing about wine but couldn't help but wonder whether we could cut back on the cost of alcohol. I knew what Sam would say and, having just decided that he knew the business much better than I, thrust that thought to the back of my mind.

I read the menu, seeking clues as to Francesca's popularity. The menu didn't seem like your average Italian restaurant—no Spaghetti Bolognese, no lasagna, no meatballs. Instead, there were Wild Mushroom Risotto and Roast Reindeer Loin.

I stood behind the door into the office area and watched the people at the tables nearest me. I watched them lean across the tables and whisper into their partner's ear. I watched them gossip with the waiters. I watched them smile as they took their first taste of whatever had been put in front of them.

And I envied them. I envied their lightheartedness, their enjoyment of the evening, their companions. I envied them their lives.

I snuck out the back around ten as the crowd started to thin. I didn't want to be in my office when the final customer left, when Sam or Melissa came looking for me. If they saw my face, they'd see envy piled on top of the raging burn.

If I was going to be the boss, I needed to quickly turn around the initial impression my employees had formed of me. I needed to get in charge and stay in charge.

It wouldn't be easy—not with Sam—but I was determined. And no one had ever stopped Heather James when she was at her most determined.

I stopped at the pharmacy on my way home and added a bottle of calamine lotion and one of antiinflammatories to my repertoire.

"No water," the pharmacist said. "It'll just aggravate the nerve endings. And touch your face as little as possible. Put on the lotion and leave it."

I wasn't sure that I'd be able to stop from scratching in my sleep. I wasn't sure I'd be able to sleep at all and that was something new for me.

Even at the height of tax planning time, I managed to get

my eight hours in. I might work the other sixteen hours, but those eight were sacrosanct.

I loved to sleep, loved slipping under the covers—soft warm flannel now that winter had arrived—and stretching out on my expensive mattress. I would curl up and fall asleep the moment I turned off the light.

But not tonight. Tonight I was stuck in a merry-go-round of itchiness and pain. Even the antiinflammatories couldn't help and I wished I'd taken Melissa up on her offer of sleeping pills.

Because if I wanted to make that good second impression, I needed to add some sleep to the slowly settling burning on my face. Red-rimmed eyes would be almost as bad as the red, blotchy face.

When I got out of bed the next morning, I ran to the mirror. Now I just looked like a boiled lobster, no longer scary red, but rather just-back-from-Mexico-and-fallen-asleep-on-the-beach-like-an-idiot red. I could live with that.

And the itching was gone, as well. So I slathered on lotion, then makeup, and arrived at Francesca's door along with Joey, Bill and Bill.

"Hey," one of the Bills said as he watched me fumbling with the key. "Just buzz for Sam. He'll let us in."

The other Bill added, "Yeah, that door always sticks. The only one who knows how to open it is Sam."

"I'll open it," I insisted, wiggling the key in the lock, gently moving the door in the frame. "Don't touch that buzzer," I warned Joey. "I'll get it."

Five minutes later, there were now seven of us standing at the as yet unlocked door. Me, the two Bills, Joey, Linda and Delores and one of the waiters.

All of them were bouncing up and down, batting their mittened hands against their arms, and watching their breath steam in the cold morning air.

"Ms. Owner," Delores said, a slight lisp softening the hated title, "can we buzz now?"

"No. I'll get it."

"It's freezing out here," Delores said, "and Sam will be waiting for us. We're going to be late."

"You're only late if *I* say you're late. Sam doesn't make that call."

All six faces wore matching looks of disbelief. I ignored them and continued fiddling with the lock. Why had it opened the first day? Why wouldn't it open now? And Delores was right. It was freezing out here.

But I wasn't going to give up. I was the owner. I needed to be able to open my own door.

I leaned against the door, the key now stuck in the lock. What I wanted to do was kick it open, just like the television cops did on every cop show ever made. The violence of the act would definitely make me feel better. I looked down at my low-heeled pumps and cursed.

"Damn," I said, "these won't work. I should have worn my Doc Martens."

"Obviously that key doesn't work. You've been trying to

open the door with that key for almost ten minutes. Are you sure you've got the right key?"

That was one of the waiters. I mentally named him the snooty one. Now I'd be able to tell him apart from the other seven. And I was pretty sure that this waiter was one of the *o*-boys. Silvio, Mario, Alberto. Whoever he was, I ignored him while surreptitiously checking the tiny cardboard tag on the key.

"Front door."

I breathed a sigh of relief, pretended not to hear the chattering teeth and the sighs behind me, and tried the door again. This time it flew open and I fell through it.

"Give up?"

Sam grinned and I wondered how long he'd been standing on the other side of the door while I made a fool of myself.

"Fifteen minutes," he said. "You've been fooling around with this door for fifteen minutes. Come on, come on." He herded the shivering staff in front of him like a farmer with his chickens. "I've got hot chocolate for all of you."

"Does he do that every morning?" I whispered to Melissa, who had shown up just as the door sprang open.

"Nope. But he won't want anyone shaking when they get into his kitchen. They'll drop stuff and he hates seeing his food on the floor."

"Oh," I said.

"Where's Mark? Don't you two come in together?"

"Yes."

"So?"

"His mom is sick and he's got no one to look after her so he's gone over to her place for the day. He said maybe he'll get here in time for dinner but…"

"But nothing. Phone him and tell him that he doesn't need to come in. We'll work something out for today." And I added *talk to Sam about staffing problems* to my list of things to do this morning. My middle of the night plan to avoid Sam Cappelletti crashed and burned because I had absolutely no idea what to do.

"But what about tomorrow?"

"I'll make some calls. Where is his mother? Maybe I can work something out."

Mark's mother was only the beginning of the day's problems. Two of the waiters called in sick. Linda spent most of the afternoon in emergency having almost sliced off her thumb. One of the Bills dropped a crate of wine glasses and I had to run to the supplier for another in between chopping, bartending and bussing duties.

"Is it always like this?"

I thanked whoever there was to thank that it was Wednesday instead of Saturday and that the final customer left at ten-thirty instead of midnight.

Sam handed me a bottle of Barolo and two glasses from behind the bar and gestured toward a table in the back.

"We don't want anyone to see that we're still here. They'll be knocking at the door begging to come in."

"Does that happen often?"

"Yes, especially with our regulars. They think if someone's still here, the restaurant must be open. And the drapes don't hide those front tables at all."

My back ached, my feet groaned in my pumps and I wasn't sure I was steady enough to lift the wine glass to my lips.

Sam pulled my feet from the floor into his lap and removed my shoes. "First day is always the worst," he said, rubbing his thumbs into the soles of my feet. "Go on, take a drink. You'll feel better."

The wine and Sam's hands massaging my feet combined to put me into blissful forgetfulness. I forgot my sore feet, my still sore face, the disaster the day had become, even the fact that, more than anything else, I wanted to fire Sam Cappelletti. I forgot that I, Heather James, owner of Francesca's Ristorante and employer of all these people, had taken over and done *their* jobs. All those things disappeared, leaving only a slight buzz and the feel of Sam's hands on me.

Sam's hands on me. What was I thinking?

I wasn't thinking, I was feeling. And feeling was a long way down in Heather James's anthology of things to do. Thinking was right at the top.

I sat up, removing my feet from Sam's lap, not without an unvoiced sigh of regret. I might want to fire him, but he did give a mean massage.

"I have to go," I said. "Tomorrow's going to be busy."

CHAPTER 7

By the time I got home, there were three messages on my voice mail.

One from Linda telling me that her brand new puppy had arrived and she was spending the day with him. She couldn't leave him alone, not yet. He'd be lonely and upset. She definitely wouldn't be in tomorrow and maybe not for the rest of the week, either.

One from Sam Cappelletti.

"Hey, Ms. Owner. We have a big party coming in tomorrow night and we'll need a couple of extra waiters. The list is in your office. You probably want to start calling them first thing."

That message just pissed me off. Why didn't he tell me earlier so I could make sure I found the extra waiters? He was trying to sabotage me, trying to prove that I couldn't run Francesca's Ristorante. Well, he might have been right, but I sure as shooting wasn't going to let him know that.

I replayed his message half a dozen times. Not because his voice turned my insides to liquid, but because I wanted to stay mad at him. Really.

Finally, I moved on to the next message.

It was from Mark. "My mom's still sick. I'm sorry, Ms. James, but I can't get in tomorrow."

Damn. That one was my fault. I'd promised Melissa I'd try and figure something out but I'd been so overwhelmed by the job—which was all new and almost impossible to me—I'd not gotten around to it.

I sat in bed, laptop where it belonged, and began the one thing sure to make me feel better. I made a list.

Number one: *Phone Sam.*

Can he get by for a day without Linda? If not, make arrangements for some kind of doggy day care and get Linda into the kitchen, if not before lunch, at the very least before dinner.

Number two: *Get to the office early and start phoning prospective waiter fill-ins.*

There was no way I could do that job. I'd done almost everything today—chopped, washed dishes, bussed tables, answered the phone and made reservations, even pulled a few beers.

But the waiters were professionals; I couldn't possibly fill in for them. Not one of the waiters at Francesca's carried so much as a notepad—they had all the specials memorized, the menu memorized—and that was a feat, it was six pages long—the wine list—another twenty pages—memorized, and most of the customers memorized.

And they remembered the customers who didn't want pepper or garlic or snails in their food, even if they'd only been to the restaurant once, six months ago. By the end of the day, I could barely remember my own name, let alone what I might want to eat.

Number two revised and highlighted. Get to the office extra early and start phoning.

Number three: *Ignore Sam Cappelletti and his magic fingers*.

Number four: *Call Mark at his mother's and find out what she needs and what I can do about it*.

Number five: *Call the Realtor and see if it's possible to sell Francesca's at a loss*.

Right now.

I turned off the laptop and the light and settled into bed, the memory of Sam's hands on me more vivid than the firing scene.

And that really worried me. Because I was going to sell the restaurant and Sam would be so angry he'd never want to see me again, let alone massage my aching feet. Falling for him was a very bad idea. I replaced the massage with the firing scene and hoped for the best.

I didn't get it.

The next morning, chaos was the order of the day. Not a

single one of the fill-in waiters was available. Half of them were already working, several had voice mails saying they were in Mexico or Spain or France for the winter, and one said, "No, sorry, I don't do big parties anymore. They're too stressful."

Worried, I checked to make sure that all my people were going to show up. Yes from all the waiters and the choppers. Still no from Mark, the answer relayed through Melissa.

Her puppy barking in the background, Linda was unavailable for work. She'd try, she said, to get in tomorrow.

"What if I find a good doggy day care? Somewhere close by so you can drop in and make sure—" I checked my notes for his name "—Buzzbomb is okay?"

"Well, maybe, but I don't want my little boy to be unhappy without me," she said.

"He won't be. I'll find the best doggy day care in the city. And I'll pay for his first two weeks there."

Anything, I thought, to keep Sam Cappelletti happy and out of my hair. Too late. He burst into my office with a sheaf of papers in his hand while I tried to head off whatever bad news he had for me.

"I have a full contingent of staff today except for Mark and maybe Linda. I'm working on Linda." I added another note to my laptop.

"What about the extra waiters?"

"No luck. Everyone's busy or away. One person isn't interested."

"Give me his name and number. I'll get him."

Red Bill hurried in behind Sam with a tray. Now, in other restaurants, I'd been told, choppers didn't normally carry trays but Sam's, as he told me over and over again, was a kitchen based on modern principles of work sharing. Everyone knew how to do everyone else's job.

That meant no one was indispensable.

I wondered if Sam included himself in that description. I was willing to bet not. The one person at Francesca's who was indispensable was sure to be Sam Cappelletti, at least in his mind.

Red Bill set the tray down on my desk and hurried back out without having spoken a word. I didn't think I'd ever heard him say a word.

"Can he speak?" I asked Sam.

"Of course he can, but he's not a man to waste words," Sam replied. "He talks when he needs to." He seemed to ponder that statement. "Not very often."

I was convinced that Red Bill was scared. I just wasn't sure whether he was more scared of Sam or of me. I suspected it was Sam. I hadn't enough power to scare anybody yet.

"Coffee," Sam said. "Pastries—" lifting the silver lid from a plate full of sweetness and using it to waft the aromas toward me. "I bet you don't like eggs in the morning so I've brought bacon, very crispy." He raised his eyebrows at me and I nodded.

What could I do? I loved crispy bacon and toast, it was my favorite breakfast.

"A few grilled tomatoes."

Okay, that was the final straw. The smile I'd been restraining since Sam first spoke the word *coffee* burst from its moorings.

I tried to wait while Sam loaded up my plate but I couldn't. I grabbed for a piece of bacon.

"Perfect," I said, "absolutely perfect."

"So are you," Sam said, his eyes on my mouth.

"Don't look at me like that. I'm not interested."

"Really?" He raised his right eyebrow and waited while I devoured half a dozen strips of bacon and two grilled tomatoes, cramming them into my mouth as if I hadn't eaten for days.

And maybe I hadn't. I was pretty sure my last meal had been sometime early yesterday because once things got rolling, I didn't have time to pee, let alone eat.

"You work for me," I finally said. "I don't date people I work with. I especially don't date men who work *for* me. Sexual harassment suit, anybody?"

"You've lost your mind, haven't you? Sexual harassment? Between consenting adults? Not in this lifetime."

"But you're my employee. I have the power in our relationship. I've seen the movies." I bit into an apricot Danish, almost drooling as it melted in my mouth.

"Are you not eating? This is the best pastry I've ever eaten."

"Thank you. And no, I'm not eating. I had breakfast long before the sun came up."

"Don't try and guilt-trip me, Sam Cappelletti. I've been in this office with the phone glued to my ear for hours."

"I know. That's why I brought you breakfast. And quit changing the subject. You. Me. Together."

The blaze of heat in his eyes almost knocked me out of my chair but I managed to hold my ground.

"No. Not while we're working together. Maybe after I sell the restaurant?"

My question sounded a bit tentative, a bit whiny, and I wanted to retrieve it. Too late.

"You won't sell this restaurant. You can't sell this restaurant. It was Francesca's life. No husband, no kids, no family. It was all she had and she left it to you."

"You're trying to guilt me again. It won't work, you know. I can't run this restaurant. I don't have the knowledge or the skills. I don't even know how to cook."

I thought about the kitchen of my condo, still as pristine as the day I bought it. The stainless steel gas stove hadn't been turned on. I used the microwave to heat up the takeout I brought home each night, the fridge to keep my Diet Pepsi and wine chilled and I'd never even used the dishwasher. Why spend the money to run it when I could wash my one fork, one knife and one plate each time I used them?

I thought of all the empty cupboards in the kitchen. I'd gone for the big kitchen knowing that it would help my resale value but my four place settings of dishes, half a dozen glasses and two mugs didn't even make a dent in the storage space.

My kitchen was as unlike Sam's kitchen as it was possible to be. And he and I were as unlike each other as our kitchens were.

"We have nothing in common," I said, out of the blue.

He raised his eyebrow again and grinned.

"Oh, *Bella*, we have plenty in common. You'll just have to let me show you."

With that, Sam picked up the tray and headed out to his kitchen while I sat in my chair and felt like an idiot. But I was kind of getting used to that because I'd felt that way most of the time since I'd first walked into Francesca's restaurant and seen Sam Cappelletti for the first time.

CHAPTER 8

Well, I'd had enough of feeling like an idiot. I was going to do what I did best. I was going to solve problems.

I found a doggy day care—Funnybones—just down the street from the restaurant. I booked Buzzbomb in for a two-week stay and went over to pick up Linda and Buzzbomb. I waited while she spent twenty minutes goo-gooing at the dog.

"Buzz, Buzzie baby. Are you gonna miss your momma? Of course you are. I'm gonna miss you, too, momma's boy. But Susie here—" the owner of Funnybones "—is going to take good care of momma's little boy and I'll be back in a couple of hours to make sure you're okay."

Susie seemed to feel there was nothing odd at all about Linda's behavior and Buzzbomb loved every minute of it. Me? I wanted to puke.

"Time to go, Linda. Sam'll be waiting for you."

I looked at my watch and grimaced. Eleven o'clock and the lunch rush was almost on us. Damn. I still needed to solve the Mark problem. I could pull beer, put bottles of San Pellegrino on a tray, find the right bottle of wine—after Mario had spent an hour running me through the list and the secret codes listed next to each bottle—even pour a scotch.

But a martini? Or a Tom Collins? I was scuppered. I didn't drink anything except wine and beer.

I added *buy a bartending book* to my list and squirmed when I begged Mario to take over at the bar for the lunch crowd. He looked down his extremely Italian and aquiline nose at me but nodded.

"Thank you, Mario. I really appreciate this. I'm working on getting Mark back."

"Work faster," he said. "I don't make any tips working the bar. One day. That's it."

I wasn't making any fans at Francesca's Ristorante—not this week. And maybe not ever. I was pretty sure that no one at Francesca's wanted me to sell the restaurant and I was pretty sure that was the reason they were snubbing me.

But I was also pretty sure they'd begun to wonder whether they'd be better off with someone—anyone—else.

I was undoubtedly the worst owner of a restaurant ever. I knew nothing about food, about shopping for it, about wine—the kind in my refrigerator came in a box—about anything, really.

I couldn't set a table. Okay, after a week I was getting the hang of it but one of the waiters still followed along behind me to straighten things out. I couldn't make a drink; I definitely couldn't cook.

And after twenty years of being Heather James, girl genius,

being at the bottom of the totem pole was more than aggravating, more than demoralizing, more than ego-threatening. It was hell.

I added *phone the Realtors* in three extra places on my list of things to do and carried on.

At least Melissa and Linda seemed to have gotten over their initial distrust. The waiters basically ignored me while the rest of the kitchen staff lived in a world of their own, seldom venturing beyond the swinging doors into the front of the house.

Sam Cappelletti hadn't changed his tune at all. He'd been angry at me on day one and two weeks later he was still in the same frame of mind. The only thing different was now he wanted to sleep with me.

And what did I want? The same thing, really, but I knew better.

Because I had already lived through this scenario and I wasn't going to do it again—I had twenty years' worth of regret and the same twenty years' worth of knowing better. It had cost too much.

Twenty-five and fresh out of college with a dozen firms trying to hire me, I was top in my class, smart, good-looking, built in a way that wouldn't let me model but more than attracted men. Especially older ones.

I was on top of the world when I was offered the job I'd been dreaming about since I knew what I wanted to do. A job with the best tax planning firm in the city and offered it by the senior partner at a dinner at the top of the best hotel in town.

What did I know? Not much of anything. I'd had my head down and my fingers flying over my computer and my calculator for almost seven years. I'd had a few dates with classmates, lost my virginity to one of them, but not one of those boys—and I used the word advisedly—could compete with Christopher James Johnson.

Christopher—no one called him Chris—was rich. That went without saying. If you did tax planning for the corporate elite, you'd better be playing on their playing field and Christopher was.

He was tanned and slim and beautifully dressed. His teeth were an orthodontist's dream and his eyes were IBM blue, the blue I looked at for most of my day. They spoke to me, just as my computer did.

And he wanted me. What could I do?

I walked right into the trap and stayed there for almost five years. Right up until the day a client came in asking for my advice instead of his and Christopher James Johnson realized that I knew way too much about his business. Way more than he did.

He dumped me. I lost my apartment and my car—both leased for me by the company. I lost my job. I lost my lover. I lost my future because there was no way in hell that Christopher James Johnson was going to give me a reference.

He thought he had me in a headlock I couldn't break.

But Christopher James Johnson was nowhere near as smart as Heather James. I had been putting money away every single month for the whole five years and I had more than enough to get out of Dodge.

I hopscotched my way across the country, stopping in small towns and big cities, trying to decide where to settle. It had to be somewhere where no one had ever heard of Christopher James Johnson.

The most satisfying thing about my trip was that I found out I could have sent Christopher a telegram within the first week which would have burst his little bubble of so-called fame.

> "CJJ? You think you're a big shot? Your fame doesn't even make it here. I'm not even out of your time zone and no one here has even heard of you. You're nothing."

I didn't send it. I didn't need to.

I continued to thank Christopher James Johnson for teaching me an invaluable lesson. Don't sleep with your co-workers. Don't even date them.

I realized after a few years that I'd extrapolated those rules just a little too far because I basically stopped dating anybody at all. It was easier. Safer. A lot less trouble.

Oh, I'd had a few affairs over the years, mostly with men I'd met on vacation. They were safe, too.

And now Sam Cappelletti, tempting me in a way I hadn't been tempted since Christopher James Johnson.

Stand your ground, Heather James. Just stand your ground.

I typed those words into my laptop and shut it down. Time to solve the next biggest problem in the daily chaos that was the restaurant business.

I buzzed the front desk.

"Melissa? Can you come in here for a minute?"

"Sure. You've caught me in the lull before the storm. Five minutes enough?"

"We need to get Mark in here before the dinner crowd. What's wrong with his mother?"

"She's got pneumonia and she won't go to a hospital. Someone needs to stay with her and she's got no other family. Only Mark."

I smiled to myself. Finally. A problem I could fix.

"Does it need to be Mark? I mean, does she want him and only him?"

"No. She doesn't even want him to be there. But we don't have enough money for home care and he won't leave her alone."

I loved the way Melissa looked at me, as if I were the only person in the world who could solve her dilemma, as if she trusted me to make everything right. No one else at Francesca's looked at me like that.

They mostly looked at me as if I were some kind of imposter wearing the owner suit. They knew I didn't have a clue. Melissa, though, seemed willing to give me a chance.

"Where does she live? I'll get in touch with the home care people in her area and have someone over there this afternoon. Two weeks' worth of home care, on Francesca's. Mark *will* come in once the home care worker shows up, won't he?"

Melissa nodded.

"Okay," I said. "Shoo. Get back to work, but call Mark and tell him what's happening so he doesn't refuse to open the door to the worker."

Once I'd arranged the home care, I carefully input the cost into my spreadsheet, together with the cost of Buzzbomb's stay at Funnybones.

Being a restaurateur wasn't at all what I'd expected. I'd expected to sit in my office playing accountant. Instead I spent most of my time putting out fires. And these weren't just any fires, they were built of flames and smoke the likes of which I'd never seen before.

Every problem was a new one, which meant I couldn't use any of my tried-and-true solutions. I had to come up with something brand new for each dilemma. I had to shift to my right brain—and that wasn't my strongest side by a long shot.

I was analytical, organized. I craved order and routine. Francesca's Ristorante was the opposite of those things. It was chaotic and disorganized and as far from analytical as it was possible to be.

Running a restaurant—running a big Italian family restaurant—required creative thinking every minute of the day. I was the wrong person for the job.

I steeled myself and prepared to brave the swinging doors into the kitchen.

CHAPTER 9

The noise, bubbly and light as I passed through the front, turned to heavy metal as I swung open the doors into the kitchen.

Sam yelled at Linda. She yelled back. Delores screamed at both of them and waiters, passing in and out, added to the din, their deep voices adding bass to the discordant symphony.

"Two linguine. One green, one Caesar."

"One veal. One chop. One special."

"Mr. Balomba is at table five. He wants his usual and he wants it now."

"Secretaries at table eight. They've got forty-five minutes and they all want tortellini and Caesars. Put a rush on them."

"Madam Grace is here with her grandson. She wants a steak, rare, linguine on the side. You know how she likes it. He wants what she's having."

I stood with my back to the walk-in freezer, trying to stay out of the way. The ballet of movement in Sam's kitchen looked like modern dance, but it was as carefully choreographed as the Bolshoi doing *Swan Lake*.

Brown Bill and Joey—members of the chorus—hauled towers of plates three feet high from the dishwasher to the prep counter. I wanted to tell them to carry smaller piles. Each time they dropped one of those plates it cost me the profit on a lunch.

"I know, I know. We make all our money on dinners. And wine. But still," I said to the freezer door, "those plates are important. Every single item in this restaurant is important."

I watched the movement around me, shrinking back into the cool metal of the door, trying to shut out the noise and the panic waiting for me as the tempo increased from a waltz to a *paso doble*.

Three-quarter time. Double time. Any minute the whole kitchen would be moving at warp speed. I couldn't keep up. The door swung open and shut, the flames on the grill leaped up and then disappeared. The knives flashed at the prep stations. The sound rose and fell as the large pots boiled, spewing steam into the air.

As much as I wanted to leave, I wanted to stay. I wanted to learn the steps of this dance.

I didn't want to cook. That wasn't in my repertoire. But I did want to be a part of it. Somehow.

Suddenly, a hand grabbed my arm and pulled me out from the wall and into the midst of the chaos.

"Here—" an apron appeared out of nowhere and wrapped itself around my waist "—take this." A cleaver—gleamingly sharp—and a pile of flat Italian parsley—I'd learned that there was more than one kind of parsley just yesterday—sat on the table in front of me.

"Chop it," Sam said. "Not too small." He held out his thumb and index finger and then laughed. "About the size of the pepper that bit you the other day."

He turned away before I could grab the cleaver and hit him over the head with the flat end of it.

"Linda. Keep your eye on her. I don't trust her with my parsley. Or my knives."

Linda smiled at me through the steam billowing from the many pots bubbling away on the range.

"She'll be fine, Sam. Look at her, she's already got it."

She winked at me behind Sam's back and then lifted her right hand and held it out with her wooden spoon arrayed across her body. She added her left hand to push down on the spoon's handle.

"Like this," she whispered. "Use both hands. That way they're out of the way of the blade and you won't lose a finger."

She pushed the spoon down, then up just the tiniest bit, then back down, moving it forward and then back.

"Don't cut too small or it'll be wasted."

The cleaver gleamed evilly at me. Obviously, it, too, knew I was incapable of even this simplest of tasks. Well, no inanimate object—no matter how sharp—was going to get the better of me.

I picked it up and tried to follow Linda's lead. She had

turned away to stir one of the pots on the range but I was pretty sure I remembered what she'd been doing.

"Up. Down. Forward. Back. Not too small. Keep your hands out of the way. Press down. Then lift up."

I was doing it.

"It works," I screamed, and didn't feel even the slightest tinge of dismay at the sound of my voice rising into the clamor around me. It felt good.

I screamed again. "Look at me. I can chop parsley. Flat Italian parsley, not just your regular everyday supermarket parsley. I'm doing it."

Linda smiled and turned back to her pots. The Bills ducked their heads and ignored me, an improvement on their usual scared fumbling when I was in the room. Sam, his eyes gleaming as brightly as the cleaver in my hand, grinned at me from the grill, flames leaping at the touch of his hand.

Damn, he was gorgeous. And he wanted me.

I continued chopping the parsley, slowing as it dawned on me. I wanted him back. And I had no idea what to do about it.

My rules had stood me in good stead for the past twenty years, kept me out of complicated and dangerous situations. Was I ready to abandon the order I'd created over the years? Was it time to let go?

My working life was complete chaos. That was becoming clearer and clearer as the days progressed. I had only the slightest control over anything at Francesca's. My role, if I had one other than as a chopper of parsley and other minor accompaniments, was as a fixer.

For the first time in my life, I didn't have a plan.

No. I did have a plan, laid out in lovely neat columns and rows on the spreadsheet on my laptop. I had columns for everything.

Staffing.

Marketing.

Reservations.

Scheduling.

I had a perfectly laid out organizational chart with a colored name in each box. My name, of course, was in the top box. Sam and Melissa and Mark were below me, then the waiters and kitchen staff, busboys and choppers. The cleaners, who arrived after midnight, had their own separate box off to the side.

But no one stayed inside their box. They were always hopping out to see what someone else was doing, to lend a hand, or criticize some action. They moved up and down the ladder without any regard for their place on the chart.

Even I found myself moving out of my box. And that was Sam's fault. He was always putting me to work at one task or another and he encouraged everyone else to do the same.

"If you need an extra pair of hands, Heather's available. She's happy to help out, aren't you, angel face?"

Glaring at Sam didn't have any effect on him. He just ignored it, his dark eyes burning holes in my skin every time he turned my way.

"Go over to the supplier and pick up a case of wine glasses. Red wine glasses. Take each one out of the box and run your finger around the rim. Make sure there are no flaws."

He demonstrated, and I swallowed the angry retort I had prepared. I watched his fingers lovingly caress the wine glass, wishing my body rather than the glass was under his hands.

Mario might say, "Table five needs more water. Fill the pitcher before you go over there."

Melissa or Linda would take a break in the afternoon, leaving me in charge of the soup pot or the reservation book.

Even the Bills and Joey got into the act. They handed me dirty plates and showed me how to run them through the dishwasher and then sat on the back stoop and giggled into their hands while they watched me struggle with the dials.

The owner-slash-manager shouldn't be chopping parsley, or bussing tables, or taking reservations. The owner-slash-manager should definitely *not* be doing the damned dishes. Even with a dishwasher.

The owner should be safe in her office at the back, counting the money on the days the restaurant was open and making plans for the future on the one day a week the restaurant was closed.

But the owner was spending her one day off shopping for new clothes.

"You can't wear a suit in the restaurant. At least not that one."

Sam glared at my tidy just-below-the-knee-length skirt and boxy jacket.

"You need to wear something more flattering. Customers spend more money if they can see your knees. And the tiniest bit of cleavage. Look at Melissa."

She waggled her fingers at me.

"We'll go together. I'll pick you up at noon."

I was being transformed, jumping in at the deep end. And I felt like I was drowning.

CHAPTER 10

Finally, a quiet day. The first Tuesday of December and as Sam had promised me, a short breathing space before the whirlwind hit. Only half full for lunch.

"Starting next week," Sam said, peering at the reservation book, "we'll be so busy we won't be able to take a breath. So whatever you do, whatever anyone tells you, do not give anyone a day off for the next month."

Oops. I'd already been petitioned by Linda and one of the waiters for some time off over the holidays. I'd said I'd look into it. Now I was going to have to go back to them and say no.

Didn't matter. I was going to enjoy my short break.

Everyone who was supposed to show up did. On time and ready to work. The only flaw was that Linda had brought Buzzbomb to work with her for the morning because Funnybones was closed. And the only safe place in Francesca's Ristorante for Buzzbomb? Yep.

The owner's office.

Which meant that every single person in the restaurant

came by. Not to check their schedule for the next week or to tell me we were running low on glasses or plates or cutlery or linens, but to see Buzzbomb, who loved every single minute of the attention.

And the only person able to get away from the restaurant to take Buzzbomb back to doggy day care? Yep. Me again.

The rest of the day, though I wasn't filling in for my staff, wasn't as satisfactory as I'd expected it to be. Instead of chopping parsley, pouring water or taking reservations, I spent the day adding the role of mother to my skill set, a role I had neither played before nor ever wanted to.

First it was Alberto.

"Heather, I need to have next Friday off. My wife's birthday. She'll never forgive me if I miss it."

"Alberto, it's December. Christmas parties, remember?"

"Yes, yes, yes, of course I remember. But I must make the birthday dinner."

"Why don't you switch it to Monday? Tell her you want to do it Monday so her friends from the restaurant can come to the party as well?"

Alberto jumped from his chair, grabbed my hands and kissed them, over and over again.

"*Bella*, you are a genius! Of course this will work."

Easy solution. Satisfied customer. The next problem was not so easily solved.

Delores, who so far as I knew couldn't speak, knocked at the door and at my "come in" hovered half in and half out.

"Delores? You okay?" I had quickly learned my role in these discussions.

"I'm fine."

"You don't look fine. You look unhappy. What can I do to help?"

Delores hovered right over to the chair in front of my desk and sat down. The story came out in bursts. Younger man. She's in love. Thinks he is, too. But she's not ready to commit and he's circling around the marriage question. Her biological clock is ticking and what is she going to do?

"Why not ask him what he wants?" I said. "Maybe he's scared to ask you. And if you find out he's not interested in commitment, you can always adopt."

Not such an easy solution. Customer not fully satisfied but left the session with a look of determination pasted on her face.

"Next," I said, raising my voice so whoever stood in the hall could hear me.

The choppers arrived en masse and I did mean mass. They took up all the space and the air in my tiny office. I could hardly breathe. I resolved that whatever they wanted, they'd get it. And fast.

"We want a raise," said Joey.

So maybe not that.

"We deserve it. We're reliable, we work hard, we do more than choppers at any other restaurant in town."

I checked the laptop for their hourly rate and their latest increase. Minimum wage. Never an increase. So maybe that.

"Fifty cents an hour. And that's my final offer."

The three of them smiled and nodded. More satisfied customers. Maybe I was better at this whole mother thing than I'd thought. Maybe I should set up as a therapist. Or put an ad in the Yellow Pages—Problem Solver For Hire. No Problem Too Big or Too Small.

I entered the raises in the laptop and called, "Next."

Sam came in and closed the door behind him. I heard the lock click over before he turned to me. The look in his eyes as he scanned my face was enough to turn it red and to heat the rest of my body to boiling point.

"Come on, Ms. Owner. We're outta here."

He pulled me from the chair and right into his arms.

"I've waited long enough. We're taking the rest of the day off."

"I can't. Too much to do."

Short sentences were all I could manage. The feel of his arms around me, the heat of his body against mine, the pressure of his erection against my stomach. Those might be the last sentences I spoke for hours.

"Heather, everyone knows you will be gone for the day."

I gulped. "They know?"

"Oh, *Bellissima*, every single person in the restaurant knows exactly what is going to happen this afternoon."

"You told them?" I screamed. "You told them we were going to sleep together?"

I pulled myself out of his arms and hurried back behind

my desk where I felt safe. Sort of. I picked up the glass paperweight from the staff schedule and hefted it in my right hand. I could really hurt him with the thing.

"Of course I didn't tell them. I didn't need to, it was obvious. Has been since the first day you walked into *my* restaurant."

He laughed. And I knew he laughed at the furious expression on my face.

"It's *my* restaurant. And I'm nowhere near that obvious."

"You are. And so am I. I have been single for a very long time, *Bella*, and my staff have been watching me. They know me very well, and you are extraordinarily easy to read."

His thumb drifted from my cheek to my lips and I reacted without thought. I leaned into him and realized again with a shock of delight exactly what he kept hidden beneath his clothes.

"Kiss me," he whispered. "I can't wait another minute."

He waited, patiently. And I considered the problems kissing him could cause. Because there was no way—once those lips had touched mine—that we wouldn't spend the rest of the day in either his bed or mine. Was I willing to risk that?

It's time to stop thinking, Heather James, and time to start enjoying. What's the worst that can happen?

Wrong question. There were way too many things that could go wrong, way too many reasons that this was a very bad idea. But I wanted to taste Sam Cappelletti and not just those amazing lips.

I thought about his hands in the kitchen, deft and fast, gentle and aggressive.

I thought about his great butt as he leaned over the counter to reach his favorite knife.

And then the old Heather James showed herself. And the analysis began. He's your employee. You can't make it through December without him. What if it doesn't work out and he walks out?

What if it *does* work out? Even more complicated. What if you're a dud in the bedroom? I mean, I didn't have a really great success ratio with men.

And what about Francesca's Ristorante? What about all those people I'd grown to enjoy and was getting to know? They were out there in the restaurant thinking about Sam Cappelletti and me…together. How embarrassing was that?

Don't go there, I ordered myself, and, for the first time in my life, gave myself up to pleasure.

I stopped thinking and started touching.

CHAPTER 11

The kiss could have blown the roof off Francesca's Ristorante. I wouldn't have been surprised to look up and see the clouds whirling above us and feel the cold rain on my upturned face.

I stepped back from him, scared and shaking. I'd never experienced a kiss like that and I wasn't sure I could stand any more. Physically, yes. I wanted it, all of it, but emotionally? Intellectually?

My mind *knew* it was a bad idea, maybe the worst idea I'd had since I went to work for Christopher James Johnson. My mind screamed, *Don't do it.*

My emotions weren't anywhere near as clear. They were tangled up like a bucketful of worms. One minute they said *yes*, the next they said *too scary, too much danger.*

And all of me—mind, body and emotions—knew the risk I would take if I leaned back into that strong body and let go. Because, after all these weeks working with Sam Cappelletti, I knew that for me it was more than physical. My emotions were involved; I wasn't so sure of his. And I'd been there, done that, paid the very expensive price for it.

I couldn't forget the restaurant and what it meant to him. I couldn't forget the look on his face when I told him I was going to sell the restaurant, grim and sad and horrified at the same time.

His physical reaction to me was obvious and flattering, but for the rest? Was he using our physical attraction to convince me to keep the restaurant? Did he want to hurt me because I wanted to sell his home? Because Francesca's *was* his home.

Maybe he had an apartment or a house somewhere, but for the amount of time he spent there, he might as well have slept in the kitchen. Too many questions, too many unforeseeable consequences.

I just didn't know what to do.

"Heather?" he asked. "Are you okay?"

I shook my head.

Sam Cappelletti often surprised me and he did so once again. He didn't slam out of the office as I'd expected, his eyes and body language angry and hurt. Instead, he turned me around so my back was to his chest and he held me.

"It's going to be okay, *Bella*. I promise you. It's going to be okay."

I wished that to be true. I really did. Because my body was perfectly willing to ignore my mind and just go for it.

"Why don't we just go for a walk? It's not raining and

maybe we both need a break away from the restaurant. I'll take you home to get changed."

"I don't think I can..."

"I've told everyone that we won't be in today, so we might as well go somewhere. I like to leave them occasionally. It's good for them to know they can make it on their own."

I wondered whether he was lying to me. Because Sam didn't seem like the kind of guy who could leave his work, his place, his people, behind. He seemed like the kind of guy who knew he was indispensable.

"I'm not that comfortable leaving them here without me."

He laughed again at that. "Without *you?* And what will you do for them? What will you do if the lamb isn't quite right or our best client wants a bottle of wine we no longer have in stock? What if the tomatoes don't show up? Or the case of extra virgin olive oil? What will you do if Brown Bill gets sick and cannot work? Will you figure out a way to replace him?"

Of course I would. That at least I could do. The lamb? No. The bottle of wine? The tomatoes or the oil? Maybe not. But replace Brown Bill? I could do that myself.

"You're right. At least partly," I said. "But I'm smart and I learn fast and this is *my* restaurant." I pounded my chest. "My responsibility. These are *my* people."

Everything I said made Sam laugh and I wondered if he was laughing at me rather than at what I said. That did not make me happy.

But I was getting used to feeling his chest move against my back as he laughed, feeling the deep pounding of his heart against my skin, feeling the tickle of his breath in my ear as he spoke. This time, he laughed so hard he snorted.

"They belong to Francesca's," he said. "To the restaurant. And I guess that means—" he traced his lips over the back of my neck "—they belong to both of us."

"Me," I whispered. "They belong to me." I wasn't sure which of us I was trying to convince.

I knew that Francesca's Ristorante would survive if I left this afternoon and never returned. If Sam left? The heart would be gone from the place.

Obviously he knew that, as well.

"You couldn't do this without me. Their loyalty, still, is to me. But, *Bella*," he said, licking the skin right behind my ear, "if you stay long enough, they will include you in it."

His lips, his tongue, his hands, were so distracting, I couldn't help but agree with him.

"If I stay long enough…"

Visions of long days and nights in the restaurant, of aching feet and smiling faces, of Melissa and Mark and Linda and Delores, of Buzzbomb. I dreamed of weddings and graduations and anniversaries, of hundreds of happy faces.

I held on to the idea of selling the restaurant in the spring and getting back to my old life, without those events, without all these people depending on me.

And I cringed at the thought of the chaos all those events,

all those people, all those problems, would bring with them. I craved order. Really.

I pulled away from Sam, dragging myself out of his arms and around to the front of the desk, each nerve in my body quivering with lust and fear.

"You've told them we won't be here this afternoon?"

"Yes. They'll think we don't trust them if we stay."

"All right. But a walk only. And I'm not that comfortable…"

He held up his hand and I knew he was grinning behind my back.

"I'll wait in the car while you get changed, okay? You'll be safe." And then he brought his lips to my ear and whispered, "You'll be safe just as long as you want to be, *Bella*."

CHAPTER 12

I spent the afternoon with a man I found so attractive just a glance his way and I started to shake. I spent it with a man who had kissed me in a way I'd never been kissed before. I spent it with a man who behaved himself like a perfect gentleman.

Bah.

I had left him in his Alfa Romeo—of course he had an Italian sports car—and climbed up the stairs to my condo. I had sat on the bed, corners tight, pillows piled just so, and thought about how his body felt next to mine.

And I decided right there and then that I was going to go for it. Why not? I asked myself. In three or four months—maybe less if I was very lucky—we would no longer be employer and employee. None of the reasons I had given myself for avoiding him would be true and I would have wasted the opportunity to spend time with the most luscious man I'd ever met.

I got back into the car wearing jeans and a sweater and carrying a rain jacket. And nothing. Absolutely nothing. It was as if he'd turned off the sex valve and turned on the *we're best friends* valve.

I tested it, turning toward him in the small front seat of the car, and touching his hand. No overt response, although I'd seen the small hairs on his wrist perk up.

For some unknown and indecipherable reason, Sam had chosen to take my words at face value. I was disappointed but consoled myself by remembering the kiss. He wasn't unresponsive, he was just careful.

"Stanley Park? A walk around the Seawall?" Sam looked up at the sky. "I think it'll be fine. It doesn't look like it'll rain for a few hours."

"I love the beach in the winter, the solitude, the silence. You don't hear cell phones or children screaming or tourists chattering away in languages I don't know."

"You don't like children?"

I wasn't sure how to answer that question but I tried to un-censor my tongue.

"I love them. But I'm an only child and I'm…" I hesitated and plunged on, "…forty-five. Too old for kids."

"Maybe, maybe not. I'm almost five years older than you and I still want to have a family. Biological or not."

I smiled out the window. Couldn't be any clearer than that, now could he? I hadn't been imagining his interest and it wasn't just physical.

Now what was I going to do about it?

I was going to spend two hours walking around the

Seawall, watching the winter shore birds, listening to the soft susurration of the waves on the beach and the harsh caw of the crows as they dropped unopened mussels from the sky to the concrete to open them.

I was going to talk to Sam about everything from our childhoods—his in a huge Italian family, mine in a perfect nuclear threesome—to the last vacation we'd taken. Mine, ever conscious of my retirement fund, had been to Seattle in March, a two hour drive across the border, where I'd stayed in the cheapest hotel that took Canadian money at par.

I had spent the days in art galleries and museums and the evenings eating takeout in my room and watching reruns of *Law & Order*.

Sam had taken a week in September and flown first-class to Paris. He'd eaten in amazing restaurants, had drank some of the most amazing wine on the planet, and had spent his days wandering from art gallery to art gallery.

He hadn't spent a single evening in his hotel room, nor watched a single minute of television.

Our lives were as different as it was possible to be. And I? I needed to decide which life I wanted.

The safe, comfortable, ordered life I'd been living since my parents died? Or the chaotic, joyous, impossible to control life I'd been living in the past few weeks at Francesca's?

I didn't know the answer. All I knew was that I wanted Sam in a way I'd never wanted anyone before.

Christopher James Johnson had been a decision of my mind. He would help my career and because of him, I would be safe. I'd have money. I'd have security. I'd have a man.

Not a man who would take anything from me except physically, but a man who would send me flowers, buy me jewelry, take me away on long weekends.

A perfect man, I'd thought at the time.

And now I knew I'd been wrong. Because Sam Cappelletti was the exact opposite of Christopher. Sam Cappelletti would never allow me to distance myself from him. Or from my own feelings. Sam would force me to acknowledge my emotions, my lust, my hunger for him. Sam wouldn't step away from me.

Could I deal with that intensity?

"Sam? Can we sit on that bench over there for a while?"

"Are you tired?"

"No, but I want to talk to you. And I can't concentrate while we're walking."

I led him toward my favorite bench. There were dozens of benches, some tucked into the trees growing out of the path, some drifting out onto the beaches that appeared and disappeared with the tide. Others, the ones favored by the seniors who walked the Seawall in the early mornings, snuggled into the windbreaks so that the sun caressed their faces and the wind left them alone.

My bench sat on a little bump off the path, three benches curving out toward the water. I sat, always, on the middle one, facing straight out toward the horizon.

Today the water shone the palest of grays. It reflected the sky back onto itself, a silver mirror, clouds moving across it in the slate light.

Sam's arm reached around the back of me, his hand warm and gentle on my neck.

"Talk," he said.

CHAPTER 13

"I want you," I said, right out loud, and then laughed at the sound of my voice speaking those words.

"I want you, but I'm scared. I'm scared because we work together. I'm scared because you make me feel things I've never felt before. What if…"

"*Bella*," he said, "don't. What if what? What if it doesn't work between us? What if you have to fire me? Or I have to quit? What if you sell the restaurant and abandon the family you love? What if you can't let go of your passion for order?

"The world is full of what-ifs. It's full of risk."

"And I don't take risks," I whispered, my voice barely audible.

"You do, you know. You take more risks than you're willing to admit."

"What?"

He grinned, pulled my legs over his, and settled me into his lap. His hands turned my face until my lips were mere inches from his.

"You kiss me in this public place. That's a risk."

"I haven't kissed you in this public place."

"Not yet. But you will."

"I won't."

But my verbal objection was as feeble as my mind was on this subject. I would risk almost anything to kiss him. On the Seawall. In the restaurant. In my bedroom—the riskiest place of all.

But I'd start right here.

It started out slowly, soft and sweet and as gentle as the wind blowing across the water into our faces. I settled into it as if I'd enjoyed Sam's kisses for a lifetime instead of only once.

The cool air heated on my skin as the kiss deepened, our tongues joined, our bodies melted into each other.

Sam was the one who pulled back this time.

"*Bella*," he whispered. "*Bellissima.*"

I took a tiny nip at his earlobe and whispered back. "Enough walking for now. We need a fire and a glass of wine. And," I said, licking the red mark my teeth had left on his ear and feeling him shudder, "I don't have either of those at my place."

"I have them both at mine."

Sam lived even closer to the park than I did. I'd been hoping I'd have some time to settle myself into the idea of making love with Sam but five minutes in the car—Sam driving as if he were on the Italian Riviera without speed limits—and we pulled up at an old brick apartment building deep in the West End.

The walk up to his third floor apartment took moments. Took hours. We stopped at each landing to kiss, to laugh at the tension in each other's face, to postpone what we both knew would happen the minute he opened the door.

The door—painted scarlet and gold—felt to me as if it were the door to a new world. A new life, maybe.

"Sam? I'm not ready," I said, my legs barely able to hold me up.

"Come on in, Heather. We'll have a glass of wine, sit in front of the fire, listen to some music."

"Not Barry White, okay? And not George Benson or Holly Cole or…"

"I told you, nothing will happen until you're ready. Look, there's the CD player and the discs. Pick what you want."

He lit a fire in the old-fashioned brick fireplace, the wood crackling with life. The wine rack next to the sofa rivaled Francesca's and he laughed at the expression on my face.

"I watch you, you know, and sometimes you turn from Heather into Ms. Owner without even a blink."

He pulled a bottle from the rack and handed it to me, saying, "Have you ever seen this label before? These aren't from Francesca's. I buy my wine one bottle at a time. Sometimes I just buy a bottle because I love the label and then, if the wine matches it, I'll buy it again."

The wine and the fire, the Yo-Yo Ma tango CD I'd put on Sam's player, combined to relax me almost into sleep.

"Tango?" Sam asked.

I didn't answer, instead reaching across the sofa to him and pulling him into my arms, touching his lips with mine. No more what-ifs.

"Dance with me," I whispered. "I want you to dance with me. I want you to let me lead."

"Of course," he said.

He trembled in my arms as I kissed his lips, his eyes, his temples. I touched the tip of my tongue to his ear, then to the sensitive skin behind it, then trailed it down his neck to the slight indent just above his collar bone.

The buttons on his shirt popped as if of their own will as I kissed down his chest to his belly, warm and rich with curly hair.

"Heather? You have to stop."

I raised my cheek and leaned it on his chest to listen to the erratic beat of his heart.

"Touch me," I whispered, lifting his hand to my breast. "Our hearts beat together."

I pulled my sweater over my head and threw it to the floor, followed by my bra. "Touch me," I said again, moving his hand to my nipple. "Touch me."

CHAPTER 14

The afternoon we spent together in Sam's apartment changed more than my sexual status.

It changed everything.

I went from being chaste and lonely and obsessed with numbers to being unchaste, overwhelmed with friends and obsessed with Francesca's.

I wanted to learn every single thing about the restaurant. Sam laughed at me, but he set me goals and each week I achieved something different.

I learned how to set the tables perfectly, how to take orders without a pen and pad, how to place the food on the table, how to sell the bottle of wine that would perfectly complement a meal. I drove Alberto crazy, following him around until I got it right.

I learned to decipher customers' hemming and hawing as they read the menu, knew when to suggest a particular dish or flavor and when to step back and let them make the decision.

I learned how to make martinis, manhattans, Tom Collinses. I learned how to judge an ounce and the exact right amount of wine in a glass. I learned how to make conversation with the lonely women and greedy men at the bar and how to make sure they didn't bother each other.

I learned how to gauge reservations. How long? When could I book the table again?

I even learned how to dress. I wore shorter skirts and higher heels and undid the top three buttons on my blouse. I couldn't make it to four, but I knew it was working when one of our regulars complimented me on my new clothes. And then gave me a big tip at the end of dinner.

The Bills, Joey, Delores and Linda guided me through the jobs in the kitchen, Sam standing at his grill and laughing as I dropped plates, cut my fingers, spilled broth and oil and butter on the floor.

But Sam's laughter no longer made me angry. I didn't imagine myself back into the firing scene. No, instead every single time Sam Cappelletti laughed at my mistakes, my skin heated, my lips tingled and my fingers curled into my palms.

When Sam laughed, I wanted him.

When he sang along to Puccini in the middle of a busy night, I wanted him.

When he put his arms around Brown Bill and comforted him when his best friend died, I wanted him. Actually, on that day, I loved him.

I hadn't told him how I felt. He hadn't said a word to me.

Neither of us had time to do more than touch hands in

passing in the restaurant. We ran from six in the morning until midnight almost every day.

I knew I'd finally been accepted as a member of the Francesca's family when Sam sent me to the market on my own in the third week of December.

"Here's the list," he said. "You know what I need."

"I do?"

"Smell," he whispered, his nose in my hair. "If they don't have a scent, don't buy the tomatoes.

"Taste," he said, his tongue sliding over the skin on the inside of my wrist. "If the olives aren't salty and pungent, try another stall.

"Touch the way I touch you, the way you touch me," he said, his hands shaping my breasts and my waist, grazing over my hips and my thighs. "Touch," he said again, his hands grasping my shoulders and turning me toward him.

It had been the busiest week of the year, Sam said, and I'd gone almost two whole days without kissing him. This kiss blew all the thoughts from my mind, the sleepiness from my head, and I wanted him with a craving that was undeniable.

Sam swept clear the desk in my office and I didn't even cringe when I heard my laptop hit the floor. I couldn't think, couldn't breathe, could only touch Sam's skin, feel his body on mine, his tongue in my mouth and his heart pounding next to mine.

"Touch," I repeated as if it were a mantra, my hands on his skin, feeling it warm to my touch.

"Taste," he whispered as his tongue did a dance on my torso.

"Look," he said, "look for flaws."

His eyes raked my body from top to bottom and grew dark with desire. "You have no flaws. None at all. Buy fruit and vegetables that look like you."

"Melons?" I asked, looking down at my breasts in his hands. "Grapes?" as my nipples peaked to his touch. "Peppers?" I giggled as I touched him.

"Listen to the vendors. They will tell you what's ripe." A sly grin crossed his face. "They will tell you what not to buy."

The early morning market run became part of my routine—which I hadn't expected. I hadn't expected Sam to give up something so important but he handed it over to me without a backward glance.

The vendors at the market called me *Bella* and Ms. Owner, interchangeably, having learned both sobriquets from Sam.

I filled in for Melissa as hostess, though I never did as good a job as she did. She had something—I learned what it was the afternoon she, Linda and Delores went Christmas shopping and left me at the desk.

"It's her smile," Mark said, out of the blue.

"What?"

The phone had been ringing all afternoon and most of the callers I'd had to disappoint. We were booked from December 20 to New Year's Eve and I didn't know how to turn them down.

"She smiles and people accept whatever it is she tells them. If she says it's a twenty minute wait, they nod and wait. If she tells them she has no space, they book for another night."

"But I'm talking on the phone," I whined. "They can't see my smile."

"That's the difference," Mark said, handing me a glass of wine and a plate of bread and cheese. "People can see Melissa's smile even over the phone."

"Please," I said. "No one can see someone smile over the phone. At least not yet," I said, but still searching for a video phone under the counter.

"Smile when you're talking," Mark said. "You've always got that pencil in your mouth and a sour look on your face."

I threw the sour look at him.

"People hear it. Really."

Every day got better, every day got easier. And I spent almost every minute of each of them waffling between selling the restaurant and keeping it.

Sam didn't push me, didn't mention it, just made sure that I kept busy and that I got to know all the routines, all the people.

"This is Heather James," he would say to a longtime customer who'd called Sam to his table to compliment him on a meal. "She's Francesca's great-niece and the new owner of the restaurant."

He introduced me to suppliers, to other restarateurs, to businessmen and hockey players and gamblers.

"She's the owner," he'd say, his smile proud.

And when he said those words, I almost believed him.

CHAPTER 15

Christmas Eve. Francesca's Ristorante closed at three and would stay closed for the longest consecutive period of time all year. We wouldn't open again until December 28.

Three and a half days off and I didn't have any idea what I was going to do with myself.

I had planned—in case I didn't get a better offer—to spend those days in my office, cleaning up the bookkeeping mess I'd left while I'd been doing dishes, chopping parsley, pouring drinks and going to the market.

But I couldn't come in to the restaurant. We had the carpet cleaners, the upholstery cleaners, the grill refinishers and the floor polishers coming—each one of them a tradition over the holidays.

What would I do for the next three days? I had absolutely no idea but I was counting down the minutes until three. I was so tired I could barely see straight and I wanted to go home and soak my aching feet in a hot bath.

I only hoped that what I did would somehow involve Sam. And I knew that at least Christmas Eve would include him. He'd warned me that the three o'clock closing was only the beginning of the day.

"It's our party," he had said a few days earlier. "We order in. Food and beer. And friends."

"We do?"

"Yes, we do. We order from the Chinese place down the street. Dozens and dozens of dishes. And beer. Plenty of beer."

"Oh," I replied, having no other response available.

"You can invite anyone you want," he said. "Invite your friends, your coworkers, your family."

"Oh," I said again.

But I had no one I wanted to invite. All of those people—my family and friends and coworkers—worked right here at Francesca's. Because I'd become part of the family and they'd become part of mine.

And that realization had made my life far more complicated.

I'd been carrying the listing agreement with me for days, trying to decide what to do with it. Half a dozen times, mostly at the end of the day when I was tired and cranky and depressed, I had almost signed it.

At the beginning of December, I'd had two wishes. I wanted only to make it through the month with my sanity. And my chef.

Three weeks later, I wanted so much more. I just wasn't sure I could articulate what that *more* meant.

I knew at least part of it was tied up with Sam and the days we'd spent in his apartment in front of the fire. Both naked hours and clothed hours.

And another part of it was even bigger than that. I wanted the family I'd found at Francesca's Ristorante. I wanted the chaos. I wanted the noise and bustle and warmth that seemed to envelop me each morning as I waited at the front door for Sam to open it.

What was I going to do?

It wasn't a tough decision, not really. Just before three, I went into my office and ripped up the listing agreement I'd been keeping on my desk.

I phoned my office and told them I wouldn't be coming back from vacation and I phoned the bank and removed half of the money from my retirement fund.

Francesca's needed a face-lift and I had all sorts of ideas about that face-lift. My new wish was that Sam Cappelletti agreed with me about those ideas.

And just before midnight, three plates of Chinese food, half a dozen beers and at least as many dances later, I said yes to Sam Cappelletti when he asked me to marry him.

My holiday wishes had all come true.

I had my sanity—Francesca's Ristorante and my friends and family there—and I had my chef.

* * * * *

Turn the page for a first look at Kate Austin's next book
LAST NIGHT AT THE HALFMOON,
arriving in stores March 2007.

CHAPTER 1

La Dolce Vita

My name is unusual, especially here on the West Coast where very few of us speak French, even as a second language. But I've learned to live with the bungled pronunciation, the incredulous questions and the raised eyebrows.

The story, which I've perfected over the years, is both simple and incredibly complicated at the same time.

It begins, as every important event in my life has done, at the Halfmoon Drive-In in Halfmoon Bay on the Sunshine Coast.

And when I say *every* event, I'm not kidding. My mother tells me I was conceived at the drive-in and I believe her.

So the story begins.

I was born in April of 1962, nine months almost to the day after the drive-in opened and six months after my parents were married in the registry office on the mainland.

They're happy, happier than most I'd have to say. I still

want their relationship to be dark and dramatic—a feeling left over from my teenage years—but it's not. They're romantic comedy, *not* drama.

While I, I am a foreign film, something indecipherable and gloomy, something in black and white rather than color. I like to say that I'm different and I want to be that way.

My name is Aimee Anouk King, pronounced Amy by everyone except my best friend TJ and my ex-husband Brad, and my parents, who choose to variously mangle the French pronunciation. I'm named after Anouk Aimee though I suspect—based on my dad's current movie preferences—he would rather have named me Gidget.

I see my mom's fine hand in my name and am only glad she didn't call me Anouk.

I live down the street from the drive-in and around the corner from Mom and Dad. I'm heading toward fifty, I have an eleven-year-old son, a very nice ex-husband, and the world as I know it is coming to an end.

I don't know if I can explain this to you, the way I feel about the closing of the Halfmoon. I never worked there—though almost every teenager in Halfmoon Bay did at one time or another. I'm not really a movie buff. I just see whatever (and I mean whatever) is on at the drive-in.

But I can count the number of Saturday nights I haven't been at the Halfmoon on my fingers and toes. A few weeks of vacation, the night Hayden was born—following, of course, in Mom's footprints when I named my child—and the one summer, the year I turned thirty, when the drive-in was closed for renovations.

So the Halfmoon Drive-In is closing and if I had the money to fight the developers for the land, I'd buy and run it myself. Because I'm not entirely sure what I'm going to do with myself on Saturday nights without it.

Hayden is getting to the age where he's just as happy to play games on the computer on Saturday night, but me? I remember the years when seven or eight of us piled into somebody's station wagon to take advantage of the carload discount. I try to forget the years I didn't have dates but went anyway with girlfriends or my parents. I think about the years when Hayden was young enough to sleep in the back while Brad and I watched the double feature, and the few years since Brad left for the mainland. In those years, I've watched Hayden, too, come to love the drive-in. And now all of those years are coming to an end.

I'm simplifying this because I don't want to admit the reality—that the Halfmoon means so much more to me than just some place to go on a Saturday night.

This sounds stupid coming from a woman who lives in one of the most beautiful places in the world, who loves her parents, whose child is perfect, and who has a devoted following for the pottery she makes in the studio in her back yard, but the Halfmoon Drive-In feels like home to me.

And I'm not sure what I'll do without it.

WHO NEEDS JUNE IN DECEMBER, ANYWAY?

STEVI MITTMAN

This book is dedicated to all the June Bayers of the world. Misunderstood and underappreciated, they are forced to bear the mediocrity of those around them with style and aplomb.

And here's to those around them, the rest of us—the daughters, daughters-in-law, sisters and others who carry on in spite of June with their heads held high, their smiles pasted on, unquestionably lovable, generous and resilient! I love you. Happy holidays!

CHAPTER 1

The First Night of Chanukah

So I'm in my dining room in Syosset, scraping last year's candle drippings off the brass menorah that used to be my grandmother's, polishing it and trying to pretend that my children don't wish we celebrated Christmas instead of Chanukah. It's hard to blame them. Christmas is everywhere—on the TV, in the stores, even on the radio. I know this last one because my kids have just turned up the volume beyond LOUD all the way to deafening so that they can be sure I hear the first few bars of "Grandma Got Run Over By a Reindeer."

After the battle their Grandma June and I had here last night, all I can think is, *if only!*

I mean really, it's not like Dana doesn't know she's Jewish just because she's singing in the middle school's "Holiday Concert" —I put that in quotes because every song but one is a Christmas song. Singing "Dreidel, Dreidel, Dreidel" is supposed to make it ecumenical. Jesse, being a ten-year-old boy who takes extraordinary pleasure in provoking his grandmother, of course told her, when asked what he wanted for Chanukah, that he's hoping for a stocking full of candy. Hey, what kid isn't? It's not like he wants to convert. He just wants candy.

And how was I supposed to answer little Alyssa, who wanted to know how come, if Santa brings presents to all the good little girls and boys, he won't bring any for her?

"Because he only brings stuff to *goyish* girls and boys," my mother told her. Like that should settle it for a six-year-old.

"Grandma Got Run Over By a Reindeer," I hear as I rub the menorah's base like a clean menorah will fix everything. "I wish," I mutter under my breath.

The phone rings and Dana and Jesse fight over which one of them will answer it. "It's Grandpa for you," Dana eventually hollers from upstairs.

I put the menorah on the windowsill and wipe my hands on the peach colored towel that matches my kitchen walls. I have a beautiful kitchen. I have a beautiful house. I should. I'm a decorator and I get to write all of it off as a business expense. Of course, I have to write it off against income, something I have very little of these days. Most of the furnishings in my house go back to my married days, when I had a father in the furniture business and a husband who worked for him.

I'd rather have an empty house…in a trailer park…next to a toxic waste dump…than still be in *that* situation.

"Is your mother over there, by any chance?" my father asks when I say hello. I'm surprised she's not at home since we're supposed to go over in a few hours to light the menorah with them for the first night of Chanukah.

"Maybe she forgot to pick something up for dinner?" It's not like she cooks. Her idea of homemade is whatever follows that word on a menu. She could be out at Ben's Delicatessen, or the appetizer counter at Waldbaums *making* dinner. I suppose she's making it happen. My father is too quick to answer that yes, yes, that's probably where she is. Except that her keys are on the table and her car is in the garage.

I'd say she went for a walk, only this is my mother we're talking about, a woman who thinks dialing the phone is exercise.

"Did you try her on her cell?" I ask him, which is a stupid question because my father lives for gadgets and usually invents excuses to use his walkie-talkie, press-a-button, see-her-face cell phone.

He assures me he's tried her several times and she doesn't answer. "I have a bad feeling," he says. I resist the urge to say that my bad feelings occur when I'm in the same room with my mother, not when she's out of view. After some hemming and hawing, he admits that he and my mother had a discussion last night. In my family a discussion means that, though it was a knock-down drag-out fight, the police weren't called and no one was taken to South Winds Psychiatric Center, my mother's home away from home. Again.

"About?" I ask.

He releases a deep, heartfelt sigh. It's his way of saying *oy*, without actually saying it. "She wants your brother to come home for the holidays."

"She wants what?" I ask, and my voice cracks. My brother, David, has been gone since he got his MBA from Harvard and my parents sent him on a vacation to the Bahamas as a graduation present. He never came back. We're talking nearly twenty years. He did show up briefly the summer before last, kind of checked the waters with my parents and found that he still couldn't stand them. Lots of yelling, screaming, huffing, puffing and finally, leaving.

"She's doing that this-could-be-the-last-year-we-are-all-alive business again," my father says. "You know, the family-should-be-together-before-it's-too-late stuff. I told her the next time she sees David will probably be at my funeral."

My father is seventy-two, and since he retired last year, he seems to be aging faster and faster. "Dad!"

"You know what bothered her? That I was going first. She wanted to know what made me think I'd be the first one?"

I'd say she did not, only I'm sure she did. If we were all forced to drink poison, my mother would insist that politeness demands she be served first.

"So then she probably took a cab to Saks and is buying herself something for you to give her when you grovel and tell her how sorry you are." My mother is not above picking a fight to get an apology present.

My father agrees, but I know his heart isn't in it. I tell him we'll be over soon, say goodbye, shout to the kids to get themselves together and, since I'm bringing it, grab the menorah and give it one last swipe. The last rays of sun stream in the window and gleam off the brass like a wink.

My parents' house is in the Five Towns. It's the ritzy part of Long Island and my mother is absolutely the Queen of Ritz. My father, much to her dismay, is the Sultan of Schlock. How they ever got together was a mystery to me until health class in the eighth grade, when, watching a demonstration of the fragility of a condom (ripped from a turquoise foil package and impaled by a banana), I finally understood why my mother coughed loudly every time my father referred to David as his *Trojan horse*.

Anyway, we arrive at their neoantebellum house with the columns and the topiary and everything but "Tara's Theme" playing when you ring the doorbell. My father opens the door to us and I can see from his expression that my mother has not shown up. Alyssa bends down and picks up the mail which sits in a puddle at his feet.

"Grandpa," she says, "you forgot your mail."

He shrugs, pats her on the head and instructs her to put it on the kitchen counter, telling her that Grandma likes to see the mail first. We follow Alyssa in, carrying a couple of bags from Boston Market that we picked up along the way, and we put everything down on the kitchen island. My father frets, asking several times where my mother could be, while I poke around in the refrigerator, surprised that my mother did nothing about our dinner.

Maybe my father is right to be worried.

"Uh, Mom?" Jesse says, fingering the stack of mail on the counter. "I think you better look at this." He taps on an envelope that has words cut out from a magazine pasted to it. It has the silly look of a ransom note. My father and I share a glance. I do the opening.

WE HAVE YOUR WIFE, it says. **TO GET HER BACK, HAVE YOUR SON, DAVID, BRING $10,000 TO THE ROOSEVELT FIELD MALL AND LEAVE IT WITH PHYLLIS AT THE ELIZABETH ARDEN COUNTER AT NORDSTROM'S. YOUR**—and then there is a picture of my father's house—**IS BEING**—and then there is a picture of my mother's watch—**ED. DO NOT CALL THE POLICE OR YOU WILL NEVER SEE HER AGAIN.**

My father blanches and steadies himself against the kitchen island. The jaws on all my children drop. I, however, smell something rotten. "Have *David* bring the money?" I say. "How would kidnappers know about David?"

"Maybe your mother asked for him," my father says. He is white as a sheet and I order him to sit down. Jesse helps him to a chair. Dana gets him a glass of water. Alyssa crawls into his lap.

Meanwhile, I look at the postmark. Yesterday. "Dad, Mom

was here last night, right?" I say. He nods. The man looks awful. I tell him to drink his water and ask Dana to see if she can't find something a little stronger.

After he's had a quick belt of scotch, I continue.

"Okay, let's look at this rationally. First off, this letter was sent yesterday, before Mom was—" I put quotation marks in the air around "—*kidnapped*. So she couldn't have told her—" I do it again with the quotation marks "—*kidnappers* about David."

I study the note. "And look at the angle of the watch picture, Dad. If I was taking a picture of your watch, I'd do it from in front of you, not behind you, wouldn't I?"

Dana and her brother are following my train of thought. My father is resisting it.

"But if I was taking the picture myself…" I motion with my hands and show my father the picture in the note.

"Grandma took it," Jesse says. Dana hushes him. My father shakes his head.

I finger the paper the words are cut from. It's heavy gloss paper from a fancy magazine. Not something kidnappers are likely to have. And what kidnappers would ask for a mere ten thousand dollars?

"You think she did this herself?" my father asks. Without answering, I go into the living room and check the glass table for my mother's magazines. Four issues of *Distinction, the Elegant Living on Long Island Magazine*, lay fanned on the table. August, September, November and December. My hunch is that October is missing a few choice words, and has been tossed in the trash.

"We should call the police," my father says. Dana reminds him that the note says not to or we'll never see Grandma again. When I catch her raising her eyebrows as if to ask if this is such a bad consequence, she looks properly chastised.

"You could call Drew," Jesse says. "He'd know if it was real or not."

Dana complains that Jesse thinks Detective Drew Scoones knows everything. I've been to bed with Drew Scoones—just once—and believe me, he does. Dana, who only suspects there was something between Drew and me, still holds out the preposterous hope that I will one day forgive her father, and while she won't suggest we call him, I know she'd like to.

Alyssa, unfazed by any of this, asks if we're going to burn the menorah and get presents. The sun is just setting. It's Friday night and we are supposed to light the candles before dark. We're running out of time to do it right.

"Yes," I tell Alyssa, furious with my mother for ruining the holiday for the kids. "And you are not going to worry," I tell my father, whose color is returning.

"Maybe we could call your detective friend?" he says. I tell him that I will as soon as we've lit the candles and given the kids their first presents.

We all go into the kitchen and Jesse holds out the box of Chanukah candles to Alyssa, letting her pick the first two candles. One will be the *shammes* candle, the one that lights the others, and the second one will signify the first night of Chanukah. Of course, with Christmas on her mind, Lys picks a red one and a green one.

I reach for a napkin to cover my head the way my grandmother taught me. I am sure that there is something more official than a napkin for this purpose, but that's what my grandmother used and my mother used, and tradition is what holidays are all about. I hand one to Dana and she rolls her eyes but places it on her head. Alyssa takes one, too, and then Grandpa lights the *shammes* with a match and no one argues that they are old enough to light matches themselves.

"*Baruch atah adonai*," we sing in shaky voices. Let's face it, with the exception of Barbra Streisand and Neil Diamond, Jews aren't exactly known for their wonderful voices. But give us a violin and we could be Jascha Heifetz. Give us another violin and we could be Itzhak Perlman. Give us a Jewish mother who will make us practice until our fingers bleed…

Alyssa takes the *shammes* candle from my father, and Dana guides her hand to light the first candle on the right.

And when the prayer has been sung, I gather the light of the candle as my grandmother did, rolling the smoke three times toward me, and cover my face with my hands while I offer up a silent prayer of thanks and praise and wishes. *I wish my grandmother was here*. And like my mother would, *I wish my brother was here*.

I purposefully don't wish my mother was here.

And then I put my hands down, reach into the shopping bags I've schlepped in from the car and hand each of my children a present. My father reaches into his pocket and hands each child a crisp twenty-dollar bill. "A little Chanukah *gelt* from me," he tells them. I'm thrilled when they thank him without being reminded. "Your Grandma has your presents but I don't know…" His voice trails off. I don't know if he doesn't know where they are or doesn't know if he should give them to the children without my mother.

Of course, Grandma June has messed up yet again. She'd told me she and my father got Dana one of those little iPod Nanos, so I got the case and all the accessories. All in purple, Dana's favorite color. Now I'm supposed to give her a Nano case to hold…nada.

I explain to her that my present goes with Grandma and Grandpa's and it's not so great without theirs. She looks at me like I'm not making any sense.

"You got the cage and they got me the hamster?" she asks. We've had this discussion ten times. She is not getting a hamster. We already have a dog who no one but me takes care of. We are not getting me more responsibilities. Besides, hamsters are rodents.

"Hardly," I tell her, and hand her a small package which she looks at suspiciously. She opens it and puts her hands up. *What am I supposed to do with this?*

"Oy," Grandpa says, realizing that their gift was a vital part of mine. "A Nano we got you, sweetheart. It can hold a million songs, almost. The man at the store plugged me in and I promise, it plays Green Day so sharp you could bleed."

Dana smiles at him with pity written all over her face. In addition to my dark hair and eyes, my pudgy cheeks and my penchant for biting the edge of my lip, she has unfortunately inherited my inability to hide a single thought behind a pleasant expression. "You think Grandma June will be home soon?" she asks.

My father looks to me for an answer. We've begun to do the dance that grown children and aging parents all over the country are learning. It's called role reversal, and we haven't mastered the more intricate steps just yet.

"Grandma may not be home until after we have to leave," I tell my eldest daughter. I give her a smile and tell her that's why Chanukah has eight nights.

"I thought it was about some oil lasting," Jesse, my smart-aleck, says. "I guess you can't believe everything they tell you in Sunday school."

"So then, you don't want your present?" I ask him, and wait for him to give the short version of the Chanukah story for Alyssa's sake. Then he takes the present from my outstretched hands. "Like Dana's," I start to say, but he gets it.

"So Grandma has my PSP," he says. "Well, cool. I mean, I'll be really happy when there's something to put in this case."

You know, my mother was so adamant about how the kids

should love Chanukah, and then she pulls a stunt like this and ruins the whole first night. If Dana had gotten the iPod, she'd be thrilled with the case. Ditto for Jesse.

I can hardly bear to give Alyssa her American Girl doll outfit because, as you may have guessed, Grandma June's gift is the damn doll.

"I'll get them the stuff they really want, and you can get them the crap that goes with it," she'd said. I'm sure if she were here now she'd be asking them who loves them best. And doesn't the fact that she's not here blow that out of the water?

"You don't know where the presents are, Dad?" I ask him.

He shrugs. "A closet? The basement?" The poor man is torn between his loyalty to my mother and making my children happy. I'm not going to make it worse. I explain the situation to Alyssa, who takes it better than I expect.

Grandpa pulls out three more twenties and hands them out to the kids over my objections.

"What's a six-year-old going to do with forty dollars?" I ask him.

"You're right," he says and pulls out more money. He hands me a wad. "Tomorrow you take her to the store and you buy her whatever one of those dolls she wants. And you get Danala and Jesse whatever they want."

I remind him that he already got the kids presents. We just don't know where they are.

"Like Grandma," Alyssa pipes up and I throw some chocolate gelt and a dreidel in the kids' direction and tell them to play.

"Maybe we should call your friend?" my father suggests again.

I hate the idea. First off, my *friend* Detective Drew Scoones already thinks my family is loopy. I mean, he knows about my mother's trips to South Winds Psychiatric Center and my own little sojourn there when my ex-husband, Rio, tried to convince me I was crazy. He knows about Rio trying to get naked pictures of me with an unconnected nanny cam he thought was wireless. He knows I kidnapped my dog from a dead woman's house and that I am a very suspicious person who seems to be a trouble magnet.

Do I really want to call him and tell him my mother's pretending to be a kidnap victim? On the other hand, if there's the slightest chance I'm mistaken, I surely want his help. On the third hand, which I could use some days, I'm not sure, but I think my mother can be arrested like the Runaway Bride for this stunt.

And unlike the Runaway Bride's family, I'm not sure I want my mother back.

And then there's the fact that I pretty much told him I never wanted to see him again. And he told me something on the order of that being too soon for him.

But my father looks so forlorn. And if I don't call Drew, he's likely to call the police as soon as we leave and I don't think I can take one more news story about the crazy Bayer Bunch.

I give in and dial Drew. I figure if he really hates me he won't pick up the phone when he sees my name on his caller ID. He lets it ring three times and then drawls into the phone, "What's it now, sweetcakes? That husband of yours need a ticket fixed?"

I tell him I don't have a husband, though he knows this because he actually took me out to dinner to celebrate when the divorce papers came through. Of course, he didn't call our dinner a date. He didn't even call the time I slept with him a date, which, since I'm convinced that he was supposed to provide a distraction while the Feds did a bogus arrest on Bobbie, my neighbor and best friend, I suppose it wasn't. That little trick is at the heart of our enmity.

At any rate, I fill him in on the situation. He sighs heavily, but says he'll be right over. I start to give him directions to my mother's house, but he snorts and says something about every cop in Nassau County having her number.

And then I remember that the note says no cops and that it claims the house is being watched, and, while I doubt it, I pass this threat on to Drew. He says he's got it covered, and adds that I should greet him like a long lost lover when he shows up at the door. "Shouldn't be too hard for you to pull that off, hmm?"

I'm pretty sure from the way Jesse is looking at me that my cheeks are turning pink. He thinks the world of Drew and nothing would make him happier than if I were to marry the man. Of course, nothing would upset Dana more than if I married anyone other than her father.

And then there's my father, who would be tickled pink if I married anyone who, in his opinion, could take care of me.

And my mother would like me to marry a plastic surgeon who would give her face-lifts for free, and Alyssa would like me to marry Bob Iger, CEO of Disney. While everyone is putting in their requests, I shouldn't forget Bobbie, who, if she had her druthers, would see me married to Manolo Blahnik.

"I'll do my best," I tell Drew, who is first on the list of Men I Will Never Marry.

Twenty-five minutes later, which means that he either used his little flashing light or showed his badge, Drew's little blue Mazda RX-7 pulls into my father's driveway and he steps out of his car with a bouquet of flowers and two shopping bags that appear full of gifts. He is, unfortunately, every bit as gorgeous as I remember him. He slicks back his hair, checks his reflection in the car window—in short, he does everything to look like a nervous lover—and then strolls up to the front door.

For my part, I step out onto the porch, throw my arms around him and give him a kiss that rocks both of us down to our socks. Well, it rocks me, anyway. He lifts me off my feet, twirls me so that my back is to the street and lets his hands cup my buttocks. Firmly.

"Miss me?" he whispers against my temple.

"Are we done here?" I whisper back, tipping my head so that anyone would think we were exchanging vows of undying love.

"What's your rush?" he asks, and he seems to grow a couple more hands and finds places to use them.

"My mother?" I say, but it's getting harder to form the words, any words. "Missing…." He runs his fingers through my hair. "…note…." He puts his arm around my shoulder. "…father…"

"Okay," he says as though he hasn't all but ravaged me, as though my knees aren't rubber and my fingers can manage the door. "Let's go in."

My father stares at us in the front hall. "That was some greeting," he says to Drew. "I wouldn't want to be in the same room with the two of you if you actually liked each other."

Drew apologizes to my father and explains that he didn't want to be taken for a cop—as if the hug, the groping, the tongue down my throat, was nothing. He throws the flowers at Dana. "These could use a drink. They've been sitting by the Peninsula Boulevard exit ramp for a week."

"I don't do water," she says, glaring at him as she hands the bouquet off to Jesse.

"Someday she'll make someone a great secretary," Drew says, to which I respond, "over my dead body."

"Let's try to avoid dead bodies, shall we?" he says. "I get enough of them at the office."

My father watches us with the patience of a saint. Must be all those years of practice with my mother. Drew suggests we go into the living room and leave the kids in the kitchen. I take Jesse aside and ask him to watch his little sister, using Dana's bad mood as an excuse because I know he'd like to come into the living room and drool over Drew. It's bad enough one of us is drooling.

My father invites us to sit on my mother's taupe sofa, even though we are wearing jeans and my mother insists that indigo dye rubs off on her cushions. I see Drew take in the surroundings. Beige, beige and more beige, with some taupe thrown in for excitement. My mother's idea of class.

My father hands Drew the note. I go over again all the signs that point to my mother being the culprit. Drew asks if we've checked the garbage. When we admit we haven't, he sends my father to look for the October issue of *Distinction*.

As soon as my father is out of hearing range, Drew tells me I should know up front that falsifying a kidnapping is a felony. I tell him I was afraid of that just as my father returns long-faced and empty-handed.

"Sir," Drew starts respectfully. "I should call this in. If you've called me here as an officer, I'm obligated to call it in. But understand that if your wife has, well, engineered this *kidnapping*, she would be subject to arrest."

"And if we called you here as a friend of the family?" my father asks, and he looks at me as if I've got Drew's handprints on my breasts and butt. "A friend with expertise, but not with an obligation, then what?"

He looks my father straight in the eyes. "Is there a doubt in your mind that Mrs. Bayer is simply trying to get your son back for the holidays? Any doubt at all?"

I tell them to hold everything and run into my father's office. I pull up Photoshop on my father's new computer but there is nothing there. I send Jesse for Grandpa and tool around while I wait, seeing what programs were open in the last day or two. What my mother may have been up to. From what I can see, someone is having entirely too much fun on the Internet, and it's not of the good, clean variety.

When Drew and my father come in, I close his IE. "Mom knows how to print pictures?" I ask him.

"You put the card in the slot. It does it for you," my father says.

Drew and I both reach for the card in the card reader. My father pushes a button. Out comes a proof sheet with lots of pictures of my children, a couple of the front of my father's house and one of my mother's watch.

"No," my father says. I can't tell if he is relieved that she hasn't been kidnapped or if he's appalled that she would put him through this. "In answer to your question, no, I have absolutely no doubt."

I offer to show Drew out. He stops in the kitchen to ruffle Jesse's hair and say hi and bye to the girls. Jesse tries to shake his hand like a man. Dana just waves and avoids any contact. Lys is twirling her hair, a sure sign that she's tired.

I walk him to the front door and we stand under the elaborate *chandelier of intimidation* my mother chose for the express purpose of assuring people that in this house, we have arrived. Of course, any sane person's first question would be to ask, have *they?*

Drew glances up, grimaces and pulls out his keys from the

pocket of the jacket he never removed. "So, once again, you didn't need me," he says. He sounds bitter.

"I'm sorry to have bothered you," I say.

"Yeah, well," he says in return. And then he looks me up and down. Just the very edge of his mouth turns up. "It was good to see you. You look good."

I tell him I appreciate his coming over and that I know my father does, too. He opens the door, but he doesn't leave. I tell him it's cold and he ought to zip up, and he asks if maybe we shouldn't go back out on the porch and finish the show. I remind him that we know no one is watching now. I'm not sure which of us is more disappointed.

"Well, so long," he says. And then he's gone. I look down and by the door are the two decoy shopping bags he brought in. I lift them and they don't feel empty. I open the door and step out on the porch to stop him, tell him he's forgotten them, but his taillights are halfway down the block.

When I step back inside, Jesse is examining the packages. I tell him they aren't really gifts, but he shows me his name on one tag, Alyssa's on another.

"Well, go ahead and open them," I tell him. "But I don't think—"

"No way!" he shouts and shows me the newest Artemis Fowl book, the one that was sold out at Borders and I'd meant to order from Amazon.com. "Cool!"

Dana and Alyssa pick up *gifts* on their radar and come into the hall. Jesse eases one of the bags toward them as he slides down the wall, opening the book as he goes, and we lose him to the Underworld.

Dana opens hers next, and while she tries to pretend it's not exactly what she wanted for Chanukah, her eyes get wide. "A boho bag," she says. "How could he know I wanted a boho bag?"

My father is standing at the end of the hall with a second glass of scotch in his hand, this one considerably bigger than the first. "What's a boho bag?" he asks.

Dana holds up a handbag big enough to carry a nineteen-inch screen TV in it and says, "this," with just a touch of reverence.

Alyssa opens hers and dances around the living room with some Barbie I don't recognize but which she claims is her absolute favorite.

My father raises an eyebrow and says he thought I wasn't seeing this man anymore, which I assure him I'm not. "But he brought presents for the kids?" my father asks.

"And you, Mom," Dana says, handing me a small robin's-egg blue box that stops my heart.

Instead of opening it, I ask my father when he thinks my mother will give up and come home. I tell him I'll bet what's in the box that she'll be home half an hour after the mall closes.

He checks his watch. I resist rattling the box.

"It's not going to go away," he says. Would that be the box, or the warmth I felt when Drew was kissing me, or the ache I felt when he walked away? "Open it."

I do.

In the robin's-egg blue felt bag which is nestled on a cotton pad inside the robin's-egg blue box tied with a white satin ribbon, is a sterling silver whistle.

The kids look puzzled. My father smiles and shakes his head. "He's no Humphrey Bogart," he says, "but you gotta give the man credit. He's got style."

CHAPTER 2

The Second Night of Chanukah

My father phoned at ten-thirty last night. My mother was still not home. I called him at midnight, figuring that when she got home they screamed and yelled at each other and forgot all about calling to let me know she was back.

She wasn't.

The phone rings at 7 a.m. "Where could she be?" my father asks. He's worried about her. And I'm worried about him. How could she do this to him?

"You've tried her friends? Roz Adleman? The women she plays Mah Jongg with?"

He tells me he's called every number in the book. "And then Dr. Cohen, too." He saved him for last? I'd have called her psychiatrist first. "I even called South Winds to see if she might have checked herself in there."

My mother hasn't been in the psychiatric hospital since the summer before last, when both of us found out we were being screwed by our husbands. Well, technically we found out that we weren't the only women being screwed by our husbands. Somehow I have managed to separate *my father* from *my mother's husband*. I don't like my mother's husband much, but I can't help loving my dad.

"A spa?" I suggest. "The Garden City Hotel?"

His answers are no and no.

I tell him we just have to be smarter than she is, and to myself I say that shouldn't be hard. We have to think like the selfish, self-consumed, willful, manipulative person she is.

"Did you try David? Could the mountain have gone to Mohammed?"

My father says he checked and he doesn't think there are any suitcases missing. Now that would indicate, in other families—assuming that there are other families in which people pretend to be kidnapped, which is a pretty big assumption—that their problem person didn't go anywhere very far or for very long. In our family it could mean that my mother planned to buy everything she needed once she got where she was going. "Her credit cards! Dad, do you get your credit card bills online?"

My father, a technophile, if not a technogeek, tells me that he gets *all* his bills online. I tell him to get to his computer, pull up whatever charge cards my mother uses and check them all for recent activity.

"Plane tickets, hotel rooms, taxis," I tell him. He tells me I'm brilliant. My father is a wonderful, astute man. Why he is still married to my mother is beyond me. "Look at everything, Dad, if you don't find those. I'm going to call Mrs. Goodman and see if she's heard from Mom."

Mrs. Goodman is the friend of my mother's who must be taking lessons from her, because she's almost as good at driving me crazy as my mother is. I am totally convinced that there is a *Secret Handbook of Long Island Rules* and "How to Drive Your Decorator Crazy" must occupy a whole chapter in there.

She tells me what time it is and I apologize for the early call, explaining that I'm looking for my mother. She tells me that it's good I called because she's ready to order her chairs and she wants them by the last night of Chanukah when she is having a big party for her whole family. If she chooses stock chairs, can she get them in time? I tell her my mother appears to be missing. She tells me that she wants standard ones, but also folding ones to match, so that as her family expands there will be room for everyone at the table. I remind her that her room isn't all that big and she tells me they are expanding it.

I ask her if she has any idea where my mother might be and she acts like she doesn't even know the woman. Three weeks ago my mother sat on the couch next to her, and Mrs. Goodman asked her opinion on every single aspect of my plan for her dining room. Now she asks if I think her drapes will be ready by Friday, too. I say goodbye without answering her and dial up my father again.

Meanwhile, my doorbell rings. Out my bedroom window

I can see the RX-7 in my driveway. Now remember, it's, like, a quarter to eight in the morning and I sleep alone. And I don't have money to waste on nice pajamas for myself at this time of year. And if I don't run down immediately to answer the door and he rings again, he'll wake up the kids before I've had my first cup of coffee and I might be forced to kill him.

I grab my robe, which is as ratty as the leggings with the holes I've got on, wrap it around me and run downstairs with the phone still in my hand. I open the door just a crack.

"I'm not dressed," I whisper, praying the kids are still sleeping and I don't have to deal with a guy I slept with once—one glorious, naive, incredible time—three grouchy children who don't like mornings, and, of course, my dad.

"Been there, done that," Drew says.

"What?"

"Nothing I haven't seen before," he says. *Nothing you're likely to see again*, I think. "Your mother show up?"

I open the door and let him in. He looks me over and tries to hide his amusement.

"You wanna…" he asks, gesturing toward the stairs. I don't know if he's making an indecent proposal or offering me a moment to collect myself, but since every fiber of my being wants both, I know I'm supposed to say no.

"Teddi?" My father's voice startles me and I realize I'm still holding the phone. I quickly fill Drew in and ask my father what he's found. "At Saks she bought hosiery and something from the coat department two days ago."

"How much for the coat?" I ask. When he tells me almost sixteen hundred dollars I rule out her going to see David in the Bahamas.

"Shearling," I tell him. "What else?" Drew leans in to hear my father for himself. He smells fresh and masculine. I haven't even brushed my teeth yet.

"Three hundred dollars in the shoe department."

Could be boots. I look down and see my big toe sticking out of my left sock.

"A hundred and forty dollars at the beauty parlor. Forty dollars at Ashley's Nails."

Bobbie, who thinks the right food can fix anything, shows up at the back door with a basket of freshly baked muffins and Drew lets her in. She and Drew have agreed to a truce, but neither trusts the other one not to hurt me. She takes in the scene, looks me over to make sure I'm all right and then hands him the basket, winks at me, and is gone.

My father is still rattling off payments for what my mother calls maintenance. The dermatologist. The Day Spa. Drew returns and leans in toward the phone to hear my father. He is inches from my face. Less than inches.

"But these were all before yesterday." My father sounds resigned. He sounds hopeless. I ask if there aren't any charges from yesterday and Drew tells me it's too soon. He brushes my hair out of my eyes as he says it and gives the two words an extra meaning which might be intentional.

Or it might not.

I never know with him.

"What about cell phone records?" I ask Drew. "Could you check those?"

He backs away from me a little and says, "Sure." My breath? The assignment?

I ask my father if he is all right and he repeats his earlier question.

"Where could she be?"

I don't have the heart to tell him that I don't know—that my mother could be *freakin'* anywhere and that I will never forgive her for doing this to him, even if she thinks he owes her. Sticking by her through everything should have been enough.

For my mother, nothing is enough.

Drew takes the phone from me and tells my father he'll see what he can find out. He asks my father again if he wants to report my mother's disappearance to the police. And he covers the receiver with his hand lightly and tells me to go upstairs and get dressed.

When I come back down, teeth brushed, hair combed and pulled back, decent clothing on, he's got coffee made, Bobbie's muffins on a plate and he's on his cell phone. He gestures for me to help myself, as if the kitchen is his instead of mine, as he writes down numbers. I glance at the list and shake my head. None of them are familiar.

He thanks his source and hangs up. Jesse staggers into the kitchen but pulls himself erect as soon as he sees Drew there.

He tells him how much he's enjoying the book and I realize I haven't thanked him for all the gifts.

"Grandma turn up?" Jesse asks. It is the same phrasing Drew used. I refuse to find any meaning in that. Drew tells my son he's working on it.

"I meant to thank you for the gifts for the children," I tell him. "It's just that—"

He waves my thank-you away and asks Jesse about Artemis's nemesis, Opal. It reminds me of that scene in *Miracle on 34th Street* when Kris Kringle talks to some little girl in Dutch and convinces Susan that he's the real deal as a result.

Only it's not just Jesse that's convinced, at least for a moment or two.

"I'll start calling these," I say, picking up the list of numbers my mother dialed yesterday morning.

The first one is Five Towns Taxi Company. The guy is pleasant and polite but he refuses to tell me if he picked up my mother and where he took her. I realize I should have simply disputed the bill and then he'd have told me where and when and for how long. I tell him I'm with the police. He laughs and hangs up.

I dial the next one and get an answering machine. It tells me I've dialed correctly—that I've reached the number in front of me—and to leave a message. I do. "Please call Detective Andrew Scoones of the Nassau County Police," and I leave Drew's cell phone number. He nods at me like I've done the right thing.

The next one turns out to be pay dirt. It's my mother's podiatrist. The receptionist tells me that my mother called to cancel her appointment for tomorrow. I decide that when we find my mother I will give her two choices—she can go to jail or back to South Winds. I call my dad and tell him what I've found out and feel my shoulders relax. Inexplicably, since I never thought she was really kidnapped, I get that itch in my nose that says tears are imminent. Drew takes the phone and makes a lame excuse for me.

"Yes, sir," he says. "She's fine. I think she's just relieved." He tells my father he's got the day off and that he'll call him later.

"Is Grandma dead?" Dana asks from the doorway when she sees me crying in Drew's arms. She says it like Grandma better be or I'm in big trouble. Drew tells her that he's sure my mother is all right, but that we still don't know where she is. Dana, who looks at me suspiciously, wants to know why I'm crying then.

"Because until this moment I wasn't absolutely sure I was right," I say. "I mean, I thought I was, and everything pointed to it, but finding out I was right made me realize I could have been wrong." Drew guides me to the table and sits me down. He starts opening and closing the upper cabinets and I tell him that the Kahlúa is in the fridge.

"No scotch?" he asks. "Whiskey? Nothing stronger?"

"No," I tell him. "And I like it with milk."

"And that'll do the trick?" he asks, surprised. I look at him like he's lost his mind, but he pulls out the Kahlúa just the same and pours it into my coffee cup. "If there was ever a house that needed scotch in it, woman, this is it."

Dana helps herself to one of Bobbie's muffins. "So what happens now?" she asks. I'm wondering the same thing.

Drew says he's going to suggest that my father report my mother missing. I ask if she doesn't have to be missing for twenty-four or forty-eight hours or something.

"For minors and people who are mentally deficient or not in full possession of their faculties, there isn't any waiting period," Drew says.

"You're calling my mother mentally deficient?" I ask. I'm surprised at how shocked I sound.

"If it walks like a duck and talks like a duck, honey, it's probably quacked."

Dana chokes on a piece of muffin and I hear Jesse snicker on the steps.

"Who are you? Elmer Fudd?" I ask, trying to be outraged.

Drew turns the tables on me. "I thought you wanted to find her, but if I was wrong, excuse me," he says, getting up from his stool like he's ready to leave.

"What about her getting into trouble for staging a kidnapping?" I ask.

He tells me that he doesn't remember hearing anything about any kidnapping. That the way he understood it, my mother went out sometime yesterday and was due back for a family dinner and never showed up. She's been gone overnight in bitter weather and my father has checked all the usual places she could possibly be.

"Couldn't *you* just look for her?" I ask. "I mean, you'd look for her if you were on duty, right? So couldn't you just—"

He explains that he is only one man.

"The idea of the police looking for her like she's some fugitive, or like she's crazy—" I can't decide which is worse, maybe because she is perilously close to both.

"She has funds?" he asks. "Enough for a hotel and a cab and meals?"

Dana assures him that no one can whip out a credit card to buy things for herself faster than her grandmother. Actually, I knew someone who could, but I divorced him.

"If she's watched as many *Columbo* reruns as your mother has, she's going to be leery about using a traceable card. Unless she has a card your grandfather is unaware of, she'd be using cash."

To me he says that he will run a check to see if any new cards were issued in my mother's name in the last few weeks. I tell him I'll have my father check their ATM records for withdrawals, but the likelihood is that my mother is armed to the teeth with twenties and fifties.

"Maybe we're going about this all wrong," Drew says suddenly. "Let's think about what June wants. She's asked for ten thousand dollars."

She's asked for my father's money, which she has equal access to. If it were about money, I tell him, she knows where it is and she knows how to get it. I rule the money out and remind him that she wants David to deliver it.

"Okay, but what did she think you two would do when you got the ransom note?" he asks. "Let me rephrase that. What did she *know* you would do?"

"Be mad?" Dana suggests. "Worry?"

"What?" I ask, since he clearly knows.

"Call *me*, perhaps?" he says smugly.

"Are you saying my mother staged her own kidnapping so that I would call you?" I don't even try not to laugh because, really, he doesn't know how funny this is.

"Hey, I'm here, babycakes, aren't I? And you told me yourself that your mother wants you married again."

"Well, yeah," I agree. "But to a plastic surgeon. To a bank president. To Bill *Freakin'* Gates."

"If she was trying to get any of *them* in your life, she'd have asked for millions rather than ten thousand, don'tcha think? Or a nose job? Or a brand new computer? What she did *guaranteed* that I'd be standing right here, right now, no?"

It is one of those don't flatter yourself moments that you feel compelled to argue with despite overwhelming evidence.

"No," I say. "She wanted to get David home and knew she'd better leave my father plenty of money to send him a ticket."

Dana agrees with Drew for the first time in recorded history. "She probably figured that that way you'd never get back with Dad."

"Oh, yeah," I tell her. "Your grandmother's plans are all

that's standing between me and a return trip down the aisle with your father. That and a lobotomy."

"Mommy," Alyssa says sleepily as she comes into the kitchen. "How come Daddy's sitting on the porch?"

I look for myself, because maybe, please God, Alyssa is dreaming. Only she isn't. Rio Gallo, the man who tried to drive me crazy and tricked me into shooting him with a paint gun which I thought was real, is sitting on an all-weather wicker chair on my front porch, turning blue from the cold.

I open the front door. "What?" is the best I can do for a greeting. I get the big Hi-Teddi, you-look-great-considering-what's-going-on-with-your-mom greeting.

I tell him it isn't his weekend and it isn't a good time.

"I can wait till your boyfriend leaves," he says, gesturing toward Drew's car with his head, which I'd like to smash through Drew's windshield.

"Just tell me what it is you want and go," I tell him. He gives me the wounded look that doesn't work anymore because, like the song says, my giveadamn's busted.

"Dana told me about your mom and I don't want you to worry about anything," he says, standing up and shrugging until he's sure his leather jacket is sitting where he wants it to, making him look damn good, even at this ungodly hour. Not good *to me*, mind you, but I've no doubt that women still find him attractive. Women with psyches begging to be wounded. "I got people out looking, people who know stuff, people who can find things out."

Drew and the children crowd around behind me. Dana is telling Rio to come in out of the cold. Jesse is glaring. I'm holding Alyssa so she doesn't go running out in her pajamas. And Drew's breath is hot on my neck.

I want to tell Rio to mind his own damn business. I want to tell him to get off my porch, out of my neighborhood, off the planet. Only the truth is that Rio could probably get the cab driver to tell him not only where he took my mother, but every last thing she said to him during the ride—not to mention her ATM code if she had him stop at the bank.

My too-handsome-for-his-own-good ex-husband puts the collar up on his jacket as the storm door frosts over. "You might as well come in," I say reluctantly. Behind me Drew lets out a heavy breath, but it isn't *his* mother that's missing. I hold open the door for Rio and tell him, "There *is* one thing you might check out."

CHAPTER 3

The Third Night of Chanukah

Last night's gifts went over like lead balloons. I don't think Grandma June was missed, but her gifts sure were. The share buds, the video game and the doll bed didn't stand up well alone, believe me. So today we are going out to spend Grandpa's money while Drew and Rio each see what they can find out about my mother.

I alternate between being furious with my mother and being terrified that she's somewhere out there, alone and in trouble. My dramatic something-is-always-wrong side conjures up pictures of her huddling in a doorway somewhere, but my for-God's-sake-this-is-my-mother side sees her in some spa with cucumber slices over her eyes.

We stop at my father's to make sure he's all right, and while I'm there I accompany him to his computer to check for any new charges showing up on his Visa statements. I pretend I don't see the 900-numbers because I don't want to know that my father is getting sex over the phone. It was bad enough learning my mother, using my name on J-Date, was having e-sex with Howard Rosen, the man I was dating this fall. Still, I suppose phone sex is better than my dad resuming real sex with Angelina, the housekeeper who all but raised me.

Anyway, the kids are searching the house to see if they can find their gifts while Dad and I search his bills.

"What's this Boats 'n Motors?" I ask my father, pointing to a line on his bill that's several weeks old. "A gift for David?"

My father says my mother doesn't know enough about boats to spend nine hundred dollars on a gift for David, but I know better. My mother could spend nine hundred dollars on a pair of pantyhose if they told her they would cure cellulite.

My cell phone rings with a death dirge. Great. Now my father is going to know that I'm on speaking terms with Rio.

"Yes?" I say when I open the phone. A picture of the devil shows on my screen, but my father can't see it because I'm covering it with my hand.

"Your mother still orbiting?" he asks.

"You have something?" I respond. My father pays attention.

"Hey. Be nice or I won't tell you what I know," he says. I hate him with every fiber of my being.

"Spoke to the cab driver," he says. "Had no trouble remembering your mother, not that *that's* any surprise."

"Rio, just give me the facts," I say, and my father gasps because now he knows for sure who I'm talking to. I give him an apologetic look and he shakes his head sadly at me.

Then he motions for me to turn up the volume so that he, too, can hear.

"No 'thank you, Rio'? No 'I know you didn't have to—'"

I cut him off, telling him I am at my father's house and that my father can hear every little twist of his knife. Thankfully, that gets him to the point.

"He picked up your mother around noon at her house."

My father confirms that at noon he was out running errands and I ask Rio if that's all he's got.

"I got more than your little cop friend did, I'll betcha," Rio says. "Never send a boy to do a man's job." I stick my finger in my mouth like he's making me nauseous and tell him to get to it. I don't need to be reminded that Drew is several years my junior—exactly how many he won't say. "She had the cabbie stop at Trader Joe's and wait for her. About thirty minutes, he says. Just imagine what that cost."

I'm busy imagining other things, like killing my ex-husband if he doesn't get to the point.

"Okay," he says. "Here's the weird part—I could make you guess, but you never will, so I'll tell you. He took her to the Marina in Freeport."

I ask if he's sure.

"Yeah. And, get this—she had a suitcase with her, so he had to help her with the bags of food and all. He brought all her stuff into some bait and tackle shop or something for her."

"Was it Boats 'n Motors?" I ask. Rio says the man couldn't remember, but he could find out for me. I don't know what my mother is up to, but I'm not sure I want Rio to know, either, so I tell him I'll get back to him and hang up.

"I hate that she made him useful," I say aloud, when I really should keep it to myself. My father agrees with me.

The kids appear at the door with forlorn faces. Apparently Grandma is even better at hiding presents than at hiding herself.

I promise them we're leaving in a few minutes and that I just have to make one more phone call. Grandpa shepherds them out to the kitchen to buy them off with rainbow cookies from the deli while I call Boats 'n Motors. I hear the same recording I got with Drew yesterday. Which means that the call she made from her cell phone the day she *disappeared* was to this boat place.

I call Drew to check in with him. He tells me that he hasn't heard back from the man. I tell him what Rio's found out and he grudgingly admits it might help. I get the feeling that cabbies at the Five Towns Taxi Company are going to be getting more than their fair share of tickets this holiday season.

I tell Drew that I have to take the kids shopping, but that I'll have my phone on. Then I reassure my father that the police are on it.

"Your friend, the detective, knows that the scumbag is in on this?" he asks. I remind him that he is in front of the children and that it's their father he's referring to.

"Ah, Mom," Jesse says while Dana fumes. "We didn't actually know that's who he was talking about."

"Well, it wasn't your father," I say lamely, not that anyone buys it.

But that's not what's bothering me. It's the phrase my father used—*in on it*. Could Rio be in on it? For the ten thousand dollars and the chance to be a hero in my family's eyes, could he have helped my mother pull this off? And does he really know where she is? Could my mother have felt that desperately about David coming home?

And if Rio is her accomplice, should I be relieved? Would Rio being responsible for my mother's safety make things better? Or worse?

CHAPTER 4

The Fourth Night of Chanukah

Well, the best thing I can say about today is that the weekend is over and the kids went back to school. From there it went downhill faster than a go-cart on plutonium boosters.

First off, Dana spent last night crying because Maggie May, the dog I snagged when I was breaking and entering a dead client's house a few months ago, is Jesse's and she wants her own furball to love. So, while I should have held my ground, I folded, as I always do, and went out first thing this morning to buy her a hamster. I let the girl in the pet shop pick it out because she had on a Green Day T-shirt so I figured she probably has the same taste as Dana. And I let her put it in a cardboard box without even showing it to me. And then I spent another eighty dollars on a hamster house and this wheel thing that goes around in one direction until the hamster goes fast enough, and then it goes around in another. And I got hamster food and hamster bedding and a headache, which I didn't have to pay extra for.

And then I got in the car and I could smell the little rodent. So add to the cost of the hamster a car wash, both interior and exterior because the car wash won't only do interiors, and besides, as long as I was going there…

At any rate, traveling with this distant cousin of a mouse on the seat next to me, making little *help me! Help me! I'm trapped in a cardboard box* noises, I thought it must be like how in England they think that dandelions are flowers, but here we know they're just weeds. Somewhere there is a civilized society where the people know that a hamster in the house calls for an exterminator.

So I got home and there I was with this, this *thing*, and I could hear it scratching in its little cardboard coffin, but there was no way I was going to take it out of there, so I put it in the microwave. But then I thought that the kids might go to make popcorn this afternoon and if they turned on the microwave they'd have guilt issues for the rest of their lives.

So I put it in the washing machine. Box and all. There is no chance anyone but me would ever use that.

As I was closing the washer lid, hoping against hope I hadn't somehow gotten a rodent with Houdini-like talents, Drew called with news. According to what he could find out, my mother may have rented some sort of boat at the Marina in Freeport. He asked me what I wanted to do about it. He didn't think set it on fire was a good plan.

Then, because I just spent way more than I'd budgeted for, I thought it was a good idea to check in with a few clients.

A couple said they'd decided to hold off until after the holidays since they'd never get delivery in time for their big family parties. They both felt the need to tell me how they love to get their families together and how amazingly all the cousins get along and on and on and on, making me feel like the only woman on Long Island who has no cousins for her children, and now can't even provide one grandma.

Mrs. Goodman asked me to come over to her house to finalize her plans. I tried to tell her that there was no way she could have her chairs in four days, but she didn't seem to be hearing me. Just like she didn't hear me the other day when I called about my mother. So I went, thinking that maybe she could read lips.

"These," she tells me, pointing at a set of chairs in one of the catalogs I left with her. "I want eight around the table and I want folding ones that match. I'll have to check with my husband about how many, but I won't need the folding ones this year, anyway. Make certain the folding ones will still be available after the holidays. Next year I'm thinking there will be more. And I'll need them then."

I tell her I'll do my best to have the eight chairs there by Friday, but that I really didn't have much hope.

"They *have* to be delivered on Friday," she tells me. "And you have to give me the delivery company's phone number. My husband insists on that."

I need Mrs. Goodman's commission desperately. It will let me finally get the toilet fixed downstairs and make a dent in my MasterCard bill, which will go through the roof, what with the holidays and the stupid hamster and all. I tell her that I'll call her with the number as soon as I confirm the delivery.

She tells me that she has the measurements for the draperies. I assure her that I always take my own measurements because that way I can stand behind their correctness.

"They're correct," she assures me.

"Yes, but if *I* measure," I explain, "and they don't fit, it's my problem. If *you* measure and they don't fit, well, the problem is yours."

She tells me that's fine. I tell her it isn't. I explain that my business depends on my reputation and that my reputation depends on clients satisfied with the excellent job I do. She says I can count on her telling everyone she knows that I've been an absolute doll to work with, considering, and that everything I did was as close to perfect as anyone can expect when they don't buy custom.

"You haven't gotten anything yet," I remind her. She tells me she loves my swatches. I beg her to let me measure and she tells me that the windows aren't there yet. All I can think is that it's like dealing with my mother. "Not here yet?"

"I'm building a bigger room," she says. "It's going to be fourteen feet, ten inches by eighteen feet, seven inches. And the window is going to be a lovely bay, six feet across by six feet high."

I ask where she's building this room and she tells me exactly where her dining room is now—they will just expand it. I tell her the configuration of the house makes it impossible to expand in both directions.

She leans back on the couch. She appears to be holding on by one fraying thread. "Just do it," she says. "Please?"

I tell her that there is no way I can get the drapes made before Friday anyway, so why don't I just work on the chairs and we'll deal with the drapes later.

"The chairs have Scotchgard, right? I have little ones coming and that's why I need the new chairs."

I remind her that her old chairs are wood and there are no cushions that could get stained, but the woman is adamant. "Don't you want this work?" she asks me. "You don't need to earn a living?"

I tell her I appreciate the opportunity to decorate her house, swear to myself that I will never work for a friend of my mother's again and leave, hoping I can get the chairs by Friday.

And somehow, on two cups of coffee and a nearly stale bagel, I make it to two forty-five. The man who runs Boats 'n Motors is apparently in the shop between three and four. The kids are due back from school any minute, Maggie May is furiously throwing herself against the washing machine, my father seems to be missing in action and the phone rings.

Caller ID warns me that it's *Newsday*. I hesitate to answer it because I've been in *Newsday* before and while the last time I was proclaimed a hero for helping foil a murder and bringing some smugglers to justice, my big claim to *Newsday* fame is that shooting of my ex-husband with a paint gun. That landed me on the front page with a picture I still hold against them.

Reluctantly, I answer the phone because who knows, maybe they have information for me. Or maybe, I hope, they just want to sell me a subscription.

"Hello?" My voice quivers a tad. Maybe they'll have pity on me.

"Teddi? It's Howard. Howard Rosen?" Like I don't know who Howard from *Newsday* is? Like there are so many men who have taken me to the Garden City Hotel for dinner? Like there is a line out the door of men who have taken an interest in my life, my children and my work? And like there are so many Howards who blew it all by trolling on J-Date and winding up trading genital measurements with my mother?

"Hello, Howard." *Forget the past*, I tell myself. *Move on*. I just can't bring myself to ask how he is without inserting the word *big* in there somewhere.

"I'll tell you why I'm calling," he says, and he sounds mildly uncomfortable. "I heard about your mother and I wondered if there was any way I could help." The man does owe me. After all, I wound up risking my own life to save his sister, Helene. Okay, so I didn't know I was doing that—I thought I was exonerating Bobbie and I never expected some thug with a gun to be waiting for me at Helene's store…

At any rate, I ask him what, exactly, he's heard. He tells me that the scuttlebutt is that my mother's disappeared. Maybe run away.

"I spoke to my editor and he is willing to put the resources of the entire paper at your disposal if there's some way—"

"—He can make a buck out of it," I finish for him. When did I become so cynical? Maybe when *Newsday* reminded the entire world about the Rio fiasco when they mentioned it in the Teddi-Bayer-is-a-hero story. I start to apologize.

Howard tells me to forget it. "Look," he says. "I've missed you. You're funny and nice and, I don't know…my heart beat faster when I was with you. I just felt good. I guess that's what it comes down to. I think of you and I smile. Even the misunderstanding makes me smile. And if anyone knows what your mother is capable of, it's surely me, so if there's any way I can help…"

I tell him that's sweet of him. I tell him everything we know about my mother's whereabouts, first making him promise to keep it all to himself. I tell him about buying Dana a hamster and how I have it in the washing machine and he laughs and offers to help take it out after work. I wind up inviting him to come for latkes and candle lighting and wonder if my mother was trying to get *us* back together with this stunt. It doesn't make much sense, but then, this is my mother we're talking about.

I call four suppliers about the chairs for Mrs. Goodman before finding one who has them in stock and can deliver them on Friday. I do a little victory dance à la Rocky around my own dining room table. I will get paid! I won't make that much on eight chairs, but it's the tip of the iceberg.

You have to look at a service business like that. You have to make your customer happy and she will come back and she will send her friends and you never know what eight chairs can lead to.

Or so I tell myself when I work out the price and find I am making a whopping one hundred and sixty dollars on this order that I've put at least a dozen hours into.

Doesn't matter. This is a friend of my mother's, and satisfying her may not make my life any better, but disappointing her would have surely spelled disaster. Again, I will never work for another one of my mother's friends.

Unless they hire me.

The kids come home from school and ask about Grandma June. I realize that it's almost three-thirty and I tell them I am calling about her now. And then I call Boats 'n Motors and get a real live person.

I explain who I am and that my mother paid him nine hundred dollars and I'd like to know what for. He's evasive, saying that what a woman does with her money is none of her daughter's business. I jump to the obvious conclusion. He and my mother must be having some sort of affair. My mother is sex-obsessed—I know my mother hasn't canceled the damn J-Date account, though Howard has canceled his. Were those 900 number calls hers and not my father's? Is my mother a sex-craved sixty-eight-year-old and is this man her boytoy? Or is he exploiting her base needs and conning her out of her—or should I say *my father's*—money?

"You didn't call back the detective on the case," I say. He hacks like a smoker. My father hates that my mother smokes. Has she found someone to develop a cancer bond with? "Are you and my mother..."

His laugh turns into a coughing fit. "She's not my type," he finally manages to get out.

"Is she someone else's type?" I ask. Before I can add that what I mean is was someone with her, he answers.

"Lady, I don't think she's *anybody's* type." He coughs again. "Sorry. I mean her being your mother and all. I guess she was somebody's type once."

"Look," I say. "My mother paid you nine hundred dollars several weeks ago and a couple of days ago she took a taxi to your place and had a suitcase and food with her. You tell me what that adds up to."

He tells me he doesn't think I'm real good at math. "Your mother rented a boat from me, okay? You happy now, lady?"

Happy? Stunned would be more like it. "It's thirty-one degrees out today," I say. "What is she doing with a boat?"

"She made me promise that I'd keep my trap shut," he tells me. I hear him slurp something and I choose to believe it's coffee.

"Well," I say, weighing my options, "my boyfriend, who is a detective with the Nassau County Police, promised me that he'd find my mother, so I'll see your promise and raise you one. My ex-husband, who knows people with middle names that are body parts, like *The Nose*—"

"And I thought *your mother* was something," the man says. "I don't want any trouble, lady."

"Just tell me where my mother is," I start. *And nobody will get hurt.*

"A houseboat," he tells me, like everyone is on one in the middle of December and I should have guessed. "She's moored in the Marina writing her novel."

Now I'm the one choking. "Her what?"

"Yeah, her next novel. That's what I said. So if you guys can't give her five minutes' peace and she's got to freeze her ass off on a houseboat in December, you got only yourselves to blame and not me."

My mother *ought* to write a novel. She's always been adept at fiction. "Did she say how long she was going to be writing? I mean, this time?"

He tells me that she is almost finished with her book, *Opus*. He says that she only took the place for a week, so he guesses she'll be done by then.

"She has heat out there?" I ask. "She's not in any danger?"

He asks me what kind of monster I think he is. "This is no *African Queen*, lady. It's a fully outfitted, top of the line, luxury houseboat. And I check on her every day, make sure the heat's not cutting out or anything. I bring her coffee—she likes that really strong stuff—and I make sure she's got what she needs. Her agent drops by every morning to go over pages and she's got a masseuse coming in every afternoon. She's writing up a storm."

A *storm*, I think as I pull the menorah down from the windowsill and place it on the dining room table, *is just what she deserves*.

I thank the man, give him my number and tell him to get in touch with me if anything goes wrong, if my mother seems ill or unhappy, if the masseuse doesn't show…or if, for any reason, he thinks it's time for her to come home. I call my father and tell him that my mother is writing a novel on a luxury houseboat in the harbor. He sputters and repeats everything I tell him, only he puts question marks on the end of each piece of information.

"She has a masseuse coming every afternoon? She's on a boat? An agent comes to see her? A masseuse?" I think he may be foaming at the mouth. I recommend we let her stew in her own juices or lie in the bed she's made or reap what she's sown or whatever other cliché he might respond well to. He tells me that he doesn't know about me, but he is taking two of her Valium and going to bed. "—in a nice warm bed, in a nice dry house, because I still have one brain cell working, which is more than I can say for your mother." He slams down the phone like I am the idiot sitting on a houseboat pretending I'm a novelist. My mother probably told old Boats 'n Motors man that her pen name is Danielle Steel.

I call Drew to bring him up to date. He acts like I purposely gave Rio the opportunity to look good. I assure him Rio couldn't look good unless they were pushing him out of a plane without a parachute.

I call Bobbie and fill her in and she has the only reaction I can relate to. She laughs her head off.

And then I look at the clock and realize that Howard is due in half an hour, I look like a refugee from an all-night grunge rave and I haven't wrapped the kids' gifts, haven't checked to see if I even have ingredients for latkes, and I'm fairly sure I don't have anything that could be regifted to Howard.

And did I mention that I have a rodent in my washing machine that is peeing through its cardboard box?

CHAPTER 5

The Fifth Night of Chanukah

...cannot be as bad as the fourth. That's all I can say. Howard kindly put the hamster in the plastic hotel I mortgaged our house to buy. I slapped a bow on it and gave it to Dana, who was ecstatic. Jesse loved the Pocket Rocket I got him on sale at Costco, and Howard thought that the toy's name was too funny for words. Even Alyssa liked *Sorry!* and *Trouble!* because, she said, she loves it when I play with her. (What was I thinking?)

Put that way it all sounds pretty good, doesn't it? Well, it wasn't. Maggie May, who I was afraid would terrify the hamster, instead was terrified *of it*. The hamster, who Dana named Furbee, started going around on his wheel and Maggie backed up across the room, got tangled in the tablecloth, yanked it—complete with the menorah and the six lit candles on it—from the table and caught her tail on fire. While we were putting her out, the rug caught fire, setting off the alarm which Howard was sure he knew how to disable before it deafened us all.

He didn't.

I thought of my mother alone on that cold boat in the midnight ink of the ocean and I envied her. I did. The idea of quiet, of no one needing anything from me, of not having to say "I'm so sorry," or "that's all right," or "this isn't how it looks" sounded awfully good to me.

Yes, the fire department showed up. Yes, Drew Scoones showed up. Yes, a piece of the rat motel burned and Furbee is loose somewhere in the house.

So. Day Five of the *Holiday From Hell*.

I call David down in the Bahamas. I think he has some phone system that blocks all calls from the 516 area code. Maybe from all of America. I get his voice mail. I tell him that our mother is hiding on a boat pretending to be kidnapped in an attempt to get him home for the holidays. I tell him that if she gets pneumonia and dies, it will be on his head. I don't say he'll be sorry, because I don't know anymore if he will be. I kind of break down at the end and tell him I could really use a brother. I think the machine cuts off the last half of my message.

On second thought, he probably disconnected it himself.

My father calls and asks me to bring the kids to light the candles. He admits it's a schlep but he promises to bring in food and feed us. I agree because, along with a brother, I could use a dad about now. And apparently, he could use a daughter.

The man has brought in enough food for an army. The Israeli Army, I guess, unless there's a Yiddish one I don't know about. He's got stuffed cabbage and stuffed derma. He's got kreplach and knishes and kasha varnishkas. He's got chicken fricassee and chicken soup. And he's munching on a pastrami sandwich to spite my mother while he's spreading his bounty out on the kitchen table. To add insult to injury, he is foregoing the placemats, which would make my mother nuts if she knew about it.

Alyssa insists that she is old enough to light the candles herself. So, after we run her fingers under cold water and put first aid cream on the burn, my father hands me an envelope. It's another cut and paste job from my mother, complete with a Chanukah stamp in the corner.

"She's upped the ante," my father says. "Twenty thousand and, if David doesn't deliver by the eighth night of Chanukah, she says we'll never see her again."

"I miss Grandma," Alyssa says. "If she was here, I wouldn'ta got *burneded*."

Jesse admits that's true. Grandma June would never have let Alyssa touch the candles in her house.

Dana takes Alyssa on her lap and reluctantly confesses that she, too, misses Grandma. "She's funny," Dana says. "Even when she doesn't mean to be."

"Maybe we should—" my father starts, but I stop him.

"Hey. She brought this on herself. And she's gone too far this time. She scared the heck out of you and she's broken the law. Look, it's Chanukah, and if the oil could last for eight days way back when they didn't even have paper to write ransom notes on, then we can last for eight days with every modern convenience known to man. If the Maccabees could do it, so can the Bayers."

Jesse, who seems to have become the family philosopher, looks at me and at his grandfather. "Oh, we can live without her here while we don't cave in to her demands," he says. "But are we going to be able to live *with* her when she comes back and we didn't?"

CHAPTER 6

The Sixth Night of Chanukah

Drew shows up in time to light the candles. He says he's practicing multiculturalism, and do I think he doesn't know what Chanukah is all about? Feeling antagonistic, I ask him to tell us all what he thinks it's about.

"Family," he says.

I roll my eyes. I've had enough of this illusive family-for-the-holidays-stuff. Mrs. Goodman spent the better part of an hour telling me how much she was looking forward to seeing her whole family. Every TV show, every ad in the paper, is full of happy families. I am overdosing on happy families. The whole idea makes me nauseous.

"You don't think so?" Drew asks. "Who was it who stood up to the Syrians and drove them out of Israel? Back then, I mean."

"The Maccabees," Dana tells him. She's learning something in Hebrew School, anyway. That is, besides the fact that she needs a custom-made dress—or thinks she does—for her *bat mitzvah*.

"And who were they?" he asks. When everyone stumbles around for an answer, he continues. "They were Judah Maccabee and his brothers. One family. And they started an army, and after three years they reclaimed the temple in Jerusalem."

"The Maccabees were a family?" Jesse asks.

Drew nods his head. I shrug. He could be right. "Family is what most holidays are about," Drew says.

"Yeah, well," I say, "not this family." I realize that I haven't lit the menorah with my brother since I was in junior high and he went off to college. My children have no cousins who want anything to do with them since I divorced Rio. What concept of family do they have? And once my parents are gone, who will they even wish they could see on the holidays?

"Do you have any sisters or brothers?" Jesse asks Drew. I realize we've never spoken about his family, though we've spent plenty of time on mine.

Drew nods and spins a tale about what Thanksgiving is like at his house. He has two brothers and a sister and a million nieces and nephews and his family sounds like he plucked them out of a holiday movie.

I am green with envy. I am sick of having a crazy family. I put my grandmother's menorah on the table, fondling the base and remembering what it was like when she and my grandfather were still alive. How they gathered my aunts and uncles and cousins and asked every year that we could be together again the next year. That was their one wish. I haven't seen my cousins in so long I wouldn't recognize them if I passed them on the street. My mother alienated them and I let them go.

I excuse myself and go up to my bedroom, where I call my father to ask him to please join us tomorrow night for dinner and some dreidel spinning. I get his machine. The message says he has gone to see June to persuade her to come home. He asks me not to be mad.

I can't help it. A tear slides down my cheek.

CHAPTER 7

The Seventh Night of Chanukah

A bleakness has descended over us. I know it sounds melodramatic, but we are all dragging around the house like we're about to come down with the flu. The kids have had enough potato pancakes and donuts and other oil-laden treats to clog their arteries well into adulthood and they are sick of them. They have had it with getting presents that require their grandmother's gifts to enjoy.

Dana has explained to me at least three times why it's better to get all your presents at one time, in the morning when you can enjoy them all day à la Christmas, than to get them in the evening, doled out one at a time, after which you have to go to bed and in the morning they are already old.

She has a point. I tell her if she wears a hat maybe no one will notice it.

She has spent the afternoon hunting for Furbee. I have convinced myself that the rodent has either gone AWOL or made a special Chanukah dinner for Maggie May. Either one is better than imagining it running across my pillow. I have run the washing machine four times and am still not convinced it's clean.

Jesse has been jumpy ever since he got home from school. He keeps checking the computer, though I don't know what for. I suspect it has to do with a girl, but only because he's getting to that age and because he keeps telling me he isn't checking for anything.

Alyssa is lying on the couch watching a video she's seen a thousand times with several stuffed animals around her, a blanket over her and her thumb in her mouth.

The sky is dark and threatening. The clouds hang low and two clients have already canceled appointments for tomorrow. The wind is whistling in the trees, which sway provocatively outside the windows.

Howard stops by. "Getting nasty out there," he says when I let him in and offer him a cup of coffee. "Your mother still on that boat?"

Jesse reports on wind velocity, barometric pressure and progress of a storm coming up the coast. Now I know what he's been watching on the Internet. I find myself buttoning my sweater.

"Grandpa will get her to come home, right?" he asks. I tell him that is exactly Grandpa's plan. I don't have to remind him, however, that Grandpa is dealing with the world's most stubborn woman.

A chair on the porch blows over, smacking against the wall and making a racket. Howard tells me he's sure there's nothing to worry about. Are there five words that strike more terror in a woman's heart than those? And these from the man who was sure he could turn off the fire alarm.

I decide it's time to take the bull by the horns. My mother has already wrecked the holiday. She's made everyone miserable and it's gone on long enough. I take the Boats 'n Motors number off the bulletin board by the phone and dial up the novelist's pal. The phone only rings once.

"Yeah?" he shouts into the phone.

I start to explain who I am, remind him that my mother is in one of his boats on the water, with a storm coming, and I'd like him to tell her she's got to get off.

"Can't do that," he says.

I admit that my mother is difficult. "Tell her it's a matter of insurance. That you'd love to let her stay, but your insurance—"

"Can't," he says.

"Look, my father's out there, too. He's a reasonable man. He'll back you up and—"

The man asks if I am sure my father is on the boat with my mother. I tell him I'm reasonably sure, that I had a message from him that he was going out there to talk to her and haven't heard from him since.

He tells me he has to call the coast guard.

"Excuse me?" I find it hard to swallow and I must look as

shaken as I feel, because Howard and Jesse are staring at me like I might fall over.

"The coast guard," he shouts, like I haven't heard him. "The coast guard. I gotta call the coast guard back and tell them there's *two* people on board."

"Because?" I ask. I feel like I'm gasping for air. I *am* gasping.

"The, ah, boat," he says, and I get the sense he's hunting for gentler words as he clears his throat. "It ah… Well, it's not in the slip."

"What's a slip?" I demand.

"You know," he says and coughs while I hold my breath. "Where it's supposed to be tied up?"

"*Supposed* to be?" I say. Howard pulls a chair over to the phone and tries to get me to sit down. Jesse yells for Dana to bring her cell phone into the kitchen.

"Now don't go imagining it's worse than it is," the man I don't know from Adam tells me. "Your mom's an experienced sailor. She's handled bigger boats than the puny one she's on."

"Oh, yeah," I say. "She's piloted the *Titanic*. Are you insane? My mother is an experienced liar, not sailor."

"Hey, she told me she had a license and—"

I ask him if he doesn't check these things. Isn't he required to actually see something before he lets an old lady rent a boat? Didn't he think it was a little odd, her wanting a boat in the middle of winter?

"Nah," he tells me. "People do it all the time. People who don't want their husbands or wives or—"

"I want my mother," I say. I don't care who else goes on this man's boats and I don't care who is doing what on them. I want my mother and my father. "Now!"

"I better call the coast guard," he says. "Why don't you call me back in around an hour, and if there's no sign of the boat by then—"

Jesse comes back into the kitchen with Dana's cell phone. And with Dana. She is arguing about using her phone when she should call her father about her missing grandmother. Jesse holds out the phone to me. "It's Drew," he says.

I grab the cell phone like it's a life preserver. "They've lost my mother," I say. "The boat isn't where it's supposed to be. The idiot who rented it to my mother doesn't know where she is and he's calling the coast guard."

Drew tells me to put on warm clothes and that he will pick me up in ten minutes. He says he will call the police down in Freeport. He doesn't tell me not to worry.

"Drew," I say before he hangs up. "My father is with her."

"On it," he says. "Dress warm."

Howard says he will stay with the kids. The big ones argue that they want to come with me. Alyssa is asleep on the couch.

I leave Howard to argue with them while I run upstairs and find warmer clothes. My first instinct is to put on overalls, which my mother abhors, and some ratty sweater and layers of things that will just drive her nuts. Instead I put on wool slacks fresh from the cleaners, a cashmere sweater that my mother gave me, a cardigan that didn't go with Bobbie's coloring and heavy socks. I hunt in the bottom of my closet and find my Uggs. They look terrible with trousers and my mother will tell me so. I find dress boots which aren't nearly as warm, but which have a nice heel.

I can't believe I'm dressing for my mother's approval after what she's done.

When I come down, Dana and Jesse are sitting with Howard at the kitchen table and except for Jesse's leg shaking a mile a minute, you would think that everything was fine.

"I called Daddy," Dana says. "He's coming over."

Howard says they've worked it out. Jesse will go with me and Drew. Howard will stay with Dana and Alyssa until Rio shows up. Then, if she wants, Dana and Rio can go down to Freeport, or Rio can stay with the children and Howard will come down. Whatever I want.

All I can think is *I want my mother*. Only that's crazy, because my mother is the problem, not the solution.

"You really don't have to stay," I tell Howard. "I'll call my neighbor." Dana tells me that there is no answer at Bobbie's house. I can't believe I haven't called Bobbie yet. I didn't think my life could ever be too busy for her. Howard says he doesn't mind, that he's glad to be able to do something to help.

And then Drew is at the door. He asks if we've got a Thermos and hot coffee and Howard miraculously finds the Thermos and fills it.

"Go!" he orders and I run out the door with Drew's arm

pressing against my back and Jesse running behind us. The rain has turned to ice and the pellets hurt my face. I pull away from Drew and huddle Jesse against me, trying to shield him from the sleet. Drew closes in on the other side and stops us for a second.

"I'm coming with you," Jesse says firmly, and Drew moves in to shield Jesse's other side.

We hurry into the car. It's dark now and the ice hits the roof as Jesse and I search for seat belts and buckle up while Drew starts the engine. As we back out of the driveway, I see Dana watching from the window, Howard behind her. He gives us a brave wave to cheer us on, and elbows Dana to do the same.

Drew tells us that the coast guard is already out looking for the boat, and turns on a scanner so that we can hear any progress they make on our way down.

Jesse sits behind me and keeps his hand on my shoulder. I pat it just as Drew pats my thigh before he rests his hand on the gear shift. He doesn't make any promises he can't keep, like that my mother will be all right, or that they'll probably find the boat before we even get to Freeport.

The scanner reports rough seas and dangerous surf conditions, with six- to eight-foot seas. Drew tries to make small talk with Jesse.

"My Grandma June is kind of a hard person to like," Jesse says. I keep my eyes on the road. The snow and ice come out of the darkness and streak toward the car's headlights like a

Star Wars light speed jump. "But there's a difference between liking and loving, and we all do love her."

I turn in my seat to stare at my son, who has put into words the lifelong relationship I have had with my mother.

Drew tells him that, while he can't promise, he truly believes that everything will be all right. And he does promise that he will do everything in his power to make that happen.

The scanner reports two downed limbs on the Northern State Parkway and Drew takes the Wantagh Parkway south to avoid them.

"I really like my Grandpa," Jesse says, and his voice chokes a little with emotion.

I try to say "Me, too," but no sound comes out.

The death dirge that signals Rio on my cell phone fills the car. I don't find it as funny as I usually do.

"Rio?" I say when I find my phone and open it.

"It's me," Dana says. "I'm using Daddy's phone. Is it okay if I leave Alyssa with Howard and come down to Freeport with Daddy? Please?"

The last person I want to see is my ex-husband. Unfortunately, he's the only father my children have, and wanting my own daddy, I can't blame a twelve-year-old for wanting hers. I tell her it's fine. Drew tells me to have her put Rio on and then takes the phone to tell him where to meet us.

It's incredibly civilized, considering the circumstances. Ten minutes later Howard calls my cell and puts a hysterical Alyssa on the phone. He apologizes profusely, but says she woke up asking for me and he can't calm her down. What should he do?

When my words don't help, I ask him how well he can drive in snow and ice. He says he'll get Lys's car seat out of my car and meet us down there. Drew repeats the directions for him.

It's looking like my mother will have quite a reception party waiting for her on the dock.

The coast guard has a little booth we can wait in. Drew talks with the man in charge and he calls the two boats out on the water for reports. They are deciding if the water is too rough to continue the search.

Rio and Dana show up. Her cheeks are streaked with tears and she is dressed like it's July, her midriff bare despite the icy cold. I take off my coat and put it around her, worried about how pink her skin is. The coast guard captain positions her near a heater, but warns her not to get too close.

Both Rio and Drew offer me their coats. I lie and say I'm not cold. By the time Howard and Alyssa show up, my teeth are chattering. He has bundled Alyssa in so many layers that she looks more like the Michelin Man than my daughter, and he puts her into my arms and then, without asking, he takes off his coat and puts it around me. When I tell him I don't need it, he simply snorts and tells me he's got an extra jacket in the car and will get it when he begins to feel cold.

The booth is small and the air is thick. After the better part of an hour, we all begin to get hot and a coat pile grows in the corner. Someone shows up with hot chocolate for the children. The boats report in that they see nothing at all.

Rio tries to amuse the children and his jokes fall flat. Snow piles up outside the booth and ice pellets hit the windows like so many pebbles.

"Do you hear that?" I say suddenly and Jesse starts throwing the coats off the pile digging for the cell phone in my pocket.

"It's Grandma!" Alyssa says, hearing the familiar *Looney Tunes* theme. "It's Grandma!"

Jesse hands the phone to me, giving me the honors. "Mom?" I say. My voice sounds like I haven't spoken in weeks.

"Where is everyone?" a deep voice responds. "I get here and no one's around. Teddi?"

I stare at the phone. "Who is this?" I finally ask.

"It's David. I'm here in Mom's kitchen and there's no sign of them. I called your place and you aren't there—you guys all go out to dinner in this storm, or what?"

"Dinner? David," I start, and then proceed to fill him in on what's going on. Tears are streaming down my face. My big brother is here. I'm not in this alone.

"Tell me how to get there," he says. To someone else he says something that sounds like hand me that pen, and Drew takes the phone and tells him he'll send a squad car to my mother's house to get him.

"We're coming in," an exhausted voice squeaks over the radio. "The waves are getting too high and we can't see two feet in front of us."

No, I think. *No*. My father has to be wrong. The next time we see David can't be for his funeral.

CHAPTER 8

The Eighth Day of Chanukah

Rio left after twenty minutes of trying to be top dog and failing. He didn't offer to take the kids.

Lys is sleeping on the pile of coats. Dana is slumped in the corner and I think she may be asleep standing up. Jesse is standing with *the men* but he's leaning heavily on Drew, who clearly wants to pace but is stuck holding Jesse steady. The room is so small that the windows have fogged over and the captain has to wipe them down with a cloth to see outside.

Halos form around two lights out on the water. They grow as the boats reach the dock—without my parents. A police cruiser pulls into the marina lot and stops just feet from the coast guard booth. My brother climbs out of the backseat. He is not dressed for the cold and his breath freezes in the air, sending clouds skyward behind him like a jet stream. He pulls his thin jacket close around him as he hurries to the door, ducking his head as if that will keep the snow and ice off him.

His hair is longer than I remember, and he is unkempt.

When he hugs me, he smells stale. It is as though I am seeing the real David, not the polished mannequin. He holds me at arm's length and tells me that he is here.

"No worries, *mon*," he says with an island accent and a wink. Then he turns to the captain and asks if there is a 7 mm wet suit around that would fit him. The captain laughs at him and says that a wet suit wouldn't be warm enough for more than a few minutes in the water.

"In the water?" I squeak, and Dana stirs but doesn't wake. "David, if they don't come back, I'm going to need you."

"Alive," Drew adds when David merely smiles at me patronizingly.

David assures me he has no intention of going in the water. The wet suit, he says, is merely for the spray. "Teddi, there's something..." he starts, but then doesn't seem to know how to go on.

"You're crazy if you think I'm gonna give you a boat in this weather, at this time of night," the captain says. "I'm not going to allow you to—"

"Look," David says. "I run the whole marina in the real Freeport, the one in the Bahamas. Boats are my business and rescues are a daily occurrence with all the tourists who think that being on vacation makes them captains for a day."

"Yeah," the captain says. "And I hear your mother's quite the sailor, too."

I assure the captain that while my mother is a liar, my brother really is a sailor. David pulls out his wallet and hands the captain a card that looks pretty official and the captain shakes his head and shrugs. "It's your funeral," he says.

"Nobody's dying," David says, looking straight into my eyes. "Teddi," he starts again, but seems to lose his nerve.

Rubbery garments appear for David. I try to stop him from taking them. "Don't go out there."

"You should listen to her," the captain says, but David just smiles a quirky smile. And now, of course, Drew decides that David can't go alone. He tells Howard to look after us, and follows David out the door. They stand outside the booth for a minute, and then David pokes his head inside and asks Howard to step out for a second.

I watch through the window the three men standing in the snow, see Howard nod, glance toward me and shake David's hand. He turns to Drew, and Jesse reaches for his coat with a jerk.

"No," I say in my take-no-prisoners voice. When Jesse opens his mouth to argue, I add, "E.O.D." It's our shorthand for *end of discussion*, as in *don't bother trying, this edict is written in stone*. I think he is relieved, and he leans down and lays his coat gently over Alyssa.

Howard comes back in, brushes away the snow that clings to his hair and shoulders like fairy dust, and ruffles Jesse's hair. "Not easy to be the ones left behind, is it?" he asks. Jesse just grimaces.

"'They also serve who only stand and wait,'" the captain says.

"You're quoting Milton?" I ask, surprised.

"Who?" he asks. When I tell him it's the poet, John Milton, he shrugs. "My sergeant in the Army always said it," he replies. And then no one seems to have anything to say.

A gust of wind sends ice pellets crashing against the windows behind us. And the three oldest members of my family are out on the water. Finally, after a long sigh, I say, "I don't know which one of my relatives is the stupidest."

Dana says something under her breath to Jesse and he nods at her. We all know who put this disaster in motion.

The men who had been out in the boats come into the cubicle, which is shrinking rapidly. They have changed into dry things, but their faces are still red and raw.

"Damndest thing," one of them says. "We checked the mooring lines and there's this rusted metal reindeer stuck on one of them. It looks like it severed at least a couple of them. It's so sharp I cut my jacket on it."

He shows the captain the arm of his jacket.

"I'm lucky it didn't take off my arm."

Jesse looks at me sheepishly. "Are you thinking what I'm thinking?" he asks.

Dana pushes herself out of the corner. "That Grandma got run over by a reindeer?"

Howard makes a quick run to a Dunkin' Donuts with Dana and Jesse to use the restrooms and pick up some sustenance. While they are gone there is a crackle on the radio and my brother reports that the waves are calmer and the snow has stopped, though I am sure he is lying for my benefit. They are headed with the current and as yet, they don't see anything.

I tell them to come back. Drew assures me that they are being careful, that they are in no danger, yadda, yadda, yadda.

I'm not surprised when the radio goes dead.

The captain tells me to go home. The roads are getting worse and he'll call me the minute there is anything to report. Howard seconds the idea. I assure them both they are dreaming. Then Howard points at my children, curled in balls on the floor sleeping.

Good mother…good daughter…good mother…good daughter. The eternal tug-of-war. Instead of monkey-in-the-middle, it's Teddi-in-the-middle.

Howard goes out to warm up the car. I struggle to get their jackets back on the children. My cell phone plays the James Bond theme.

"Radio's out," Drew says. "We see something. Hang tight."

"What do you see?" I scream into the phone, and the children startle. Jesse is instantly alert, Dana, less so.

"Houseboat, maybe," Drew says. "Lights on. Weird shape."

He seems to think he's sending a telegram and can only speak in partial sentences.

"Is it them?"

He says he's got to help David and that they'll call back. Howard by now is back, ready to carry the kids to the car. I tell him what's happened and he goes back out into the snow to turn off the car. When he returns, Alyssa wakes up and announces that she has to go to the bathroom. Howard offers to make another Dunkin' Donuts run. The man is a saint.

The captain asks how long we've been married. Jesse and Dana jump on him, assuring him that we aren't. At the moment, as I watch tall, strong Howard carry Alyssa to his beautiful Mercedes where she may wind up peeing on the leather seat, I think the idea sounds lovely.

James Bond sounds again, and I realize that the man calling is risking his life for my crazy family and I feel disloyal for even thinking that Howard is nice.

Not that I want either man in my bed or my life. Long term, that is. Permanently affixed to me like a barnacle.

"Hello?" I say into the phone.

"It's them. They look fine from here. It'll take a while to work out the logistics, but I think you can breathe again."

I gulp in an enormous breath, a breath so big it makes me light-headed.

"You okay?" the captain asks me. "You look sorta funny."

"Maybe you need some air," Dana says, and Jesse opens and closes the door several times, fanning me with cold air and watching me like a hawk.

"Mom? Are you gonna faint?" he asks.

"She always does this," Dana tells the captain. "She's great until things seem to be okay. Then she falls apart."

I tell her that I am not falling apart. I say this as I grip, white-knuckled, the wooden ledge I've been leaning against.

Behind my left eye, one of those big Chinese gongs is being struck by a huge mallet. Its echo reverberates in my temple and along my jaw. It is struck again and again.

After what feels like hours, Howard shows up with strong black coffee and we fill him in while he unwraps Alyssa and lays her back down on the reestablished coat pile.

And we wait.

Every now and then one of the kids asks how long it's been. Minutes crawl.

"Five minutes later than the last time you asked."

I begin to think my watch is broken and check the one on Howard's wrist. He lets me angle his arm so that I can see it is exactly the same time on his watch as it is on mine. And then he puts an arm around me.

"Call Drew," Dana says, but we all decide that he probably has his hands full and wouldn't answer anyway. And that would make us worry *more*, if there is a more after *with every breath*.

I ask Howard what it was that David told him before he left, and Howard says that David just instructed him to take care of me. But he hesitates before he says it and I know that there was more. Howard admits there was something else, but says it is one of those in-the-event-of-my-death-open-this-letter sort of things.

We all stare at him when he mentions the *D* word.

And then James Bond plays again. I wonder for a moment if Howard is curious about his own ring tone on my phone and realize that I never gave him one. This is not something to ponder now, as I flip open the phone and hear my father's voice.

"Teddi? Teddi, can you hear me?"

I nod vigorously, but, of course, he can't hear that. I seem unable to find my voice. Jesse grabs the phone from my hands.

"It's me, Grandpa. Jesse," he shouts. "Are you all right? Is Grandma?"

"We're fine," he says, but his voice shakes badly.

Apparently Drew takes the phone from him and asks for me. Him I can talk to. "They're wet, they're cold and they're shaken up," he tells me. "But they're safe. We're heading in."

"Thank you," I say. My voice comes out a whisper.

"No problem," he tosses back, like he's picked up my newspaper from the floor, or taken the milk out of the fridge or changed a burned-out bulb.

The captain makes a call to EMS and by the time we see the boat's small beam on the water there is a truck with flashing lights waiting in the parking lot to make sure my parents are all right.

I watch as Drew and David help my father out of the boat and steady him onto the dock. He moves like the old man I sometimes forget he is. They carry my mother between them. Someone from EMS wraps my father in a silver blanket. A gurney appears for my mother. I realize the snow has stopped.

David walks past both of them and meets me halfway down the pier. He tells me he is sorry.

"For what?" I ask, brushing frozen foam off his hair and wondering when the last time I touched him was. "You were wonderful. You—"

"For leaving you holding the bag. It was a coward's way out, and I took it." I start to say something, though I don't know what it ought to be, but he continues. "They make me crazy. I was ready to throw her overboard after ten minutes of trying to save her life."

Relief. That's what I feel. She's all right. She must be, or her *crazy rate* would have at least slowed, wouldn't it?

"She was telling us how to tie the lines together. She wasn't sure her shoes matched her outfit. She wanted Dad to go back and get her damn purse."

I can't help smiling.

My mother got her wish. My brother is home for the holidays. A very nice young man from EMS tells me that my parents have refused to go to the hospital to be checked out. He tells me that they appear to be surprisingly well, considering their ordeal.

He recommends that we take them straight home and get them out of their wet clothes, check their fingers and toes carefully and—provided the digits are flesh-colored—give them warm but not hot showers, get them into dry clothes, and put them to bed.

We start to figure out who will go in which car. My mother demands David, who warns her that if the ocean didn't kill her, he just might. Howard offers to take the kids back to my house, which leaves Drew, who seems to feel superfluous, to take the rest of us back to my parents' house. Then the drivers and cars get reversed because my mother wants to ride in the Mercedes, not the Mazda, and the grown-ups can fit in the Mercedes and the kids can fit in the Mazda.

Howard offers to drop us off and then return to relieve Drew, who won't hear of it. He claims to be fine looking after the children—who naturally insist they don't need looking after.

Since my mother is shivering, we don't do the usual arguing. Drew takes off for my place with the kids. Howard takes us to my parents'.

David is silent for the entire twenty minute slosh through the snow. He stares out the window as if he can't believe any of it—that he's in New York, that it's snowing, that he's rescued my parents, that he's returning home.

Finally, when he senses we are near the house, he speaks.

"I brought someone with me," he says. I had thought my mother was asleep, but her eyes fly open at this announcement.

"*Someone?*" Howard says. "Count again." And I realize that this is what David told him before he went to rescue my parents. *In the event that we don't come back, there's someone waiting at my parents' house…*

I see David smile. "Right. Actually, two *someones*." I think about how David smelled when he first hugged me and find

I am smiling, too. Sitting in the backseat between David and my father, I grasp both their hands and wish I had another pair of arms with which to hug myself.

It is agreed that my mother deserves to be punished, not rewarded. Under the guise of doctor's orders, we have insisted she be confined to bed for twenty-four hours. We have all threatened to leave if she sets a foot outside her room.

All except her new daughter-in-law, who finds it hysterically amusing that my mother thinks that she is domestic help brought by David to make her life easier.

"He couldn't be interested in an Island girl," my mother tells me when Isolde takes my mother's tray and leaves the room. "Unless it was Long Island."

Isolde, who has a sense of humor my brother never possessed, refuses to tell my mother the truth. She claims my mother has had enough of a shock for the day, but the twinkle in her dark eyes tells me that Issie guessed June would make the assumption she has—and that she has a bet going with David about how long they can keep it up.

Meanwhile, my children, who Howard brought over, are entertaining their new baby cousin in the den, where June can't hear his little squeals of joy. Howard is staying for dinner, a reward for not only all the help he gave us last night, but for finding Furbee and buying him a new condo which we will keep in the basement, where Maggie May is not allowed to go. Drew apparently repaired the burned one by reconfiguring it. That one will stay in Dana's room for the times she wants the rodent to keep her company. She's changed his name to Donald Trump, now that he has two homes.

Drew is here, too. He claims he just stopped by to check on how my parents are doing and to *close the case*, but I think he wanted to see if Howard was invited to dinner. Jesse, of course, rushed to invite him to stay.

So we are nine, not counting baby Cody or my mother, since neither will have a place set for them at the table.

Isolde and I carry plates into the dining room and I realize that the chairs around the table are new. "Son of a bitch!" I say and then cover my mouth because there are kids around. These are the chairs I bought for Mrs. Goodman. The ones my mother had a hand in picking out. I leave Issie bewildered and storm upstairs.

"The chairs," I say to my mother and she gives me that you-didn't-fall-for-my-little-ploy-did-you flutter of the eyelids.

She sits upright in her bed, propped up by four or five pillows in various shades of taupe. "You'd never have taken your commission if I'd asked you to get them for me, right?"

Well, of course, right. And it's hard to be mad at her for trying to get me to take money.

"And," she adds imperiously, "for me, you'd never have gotten them on time, would you?"

Well, true, too. I'd have told her I couldn't get them so

quickly and ordered them through another source that would have saved her some money.

"And," she says with her nose stuck so far up in the air that even with her mouth closed I can still see down her throat, "I do need extra chairs, don't I? David did come, didn't he?"

It's like she has a needle meter and always goes just one decibel too far. "Too bad you can't enjoy the chairs or the visit," I say.

"Why is everyone being so mean to me after the ordeal I've been through? What's the matter with you people?"

I tell her that maybe, just maybe, we are fed up with her antics and faking a kidnapping went over the line. "Daddy could have had a heart attack," I tell her.

"And I couldn't?" she asks, eyes wide. Well, of course they are—she's had two eye lifts. "I could have died out on that boat and no one would have known."

"And whose fault is that?" I ask. "Yours."

She stares at me for a while. I think she's trying to narrow her eyes, but with all the Botox and surgeries, nothing happens. "Besides," she says, "you don't know what happened out there. Maybe I convinced the kidnappers to let me go. Maybe I threw them overboard."

"If that's the case," a deep male voice says from behind me, and I whirl around to see Drew in the doorway, "I'll have to take you in and book you."

"Self-defense," my mother shouts at us. "What about self-defense?"

"Don't talk to me about self-defense," I tell her. "I've been practicing it my whole life."

She tells me that by now I ought to be perfect at it, then. Drew bows out gracefully, squeezing my arm before he leaves in a gesture that shouts *be strong!*

My mother picks at imaginary specks on her comforter. Just when I'm feeling bad for her and thinking she doesn't really want to be the way she is, she tells me that she's decided to have her dinner brought on a tray, as her ordeal was just too great to go downstairs. Hey, if she wants to pretend it's her choice, she's not fooling anyone but herself. "Tell the maid I'm ready for my dinner."

I bite my tongue because I've promised Issie, and I throw up my hands as I turn on my heel and walk out her door. I bump into David in the hall.

"I'm going to straighten her out," David tells me.

"Well," I warn him, "she's flying high on her victory." I tell him how she's gloating over having made him come home.

David looks at me like I've got a screw loose. Trust me, I know that look by now. "Leave it to our mother to think I came home for her," he says. "I've only refused her a million times."

"But this time you came," I remind him.

He touches the tip of my nose, senses that I hate that little gesture and rocks back on his heels. "This time *you* asked."

"Well yes, for *her*," I say.

He shakes his head. "You said that *you* needed me." He

raises my chin with his finger. "You never asked me to come home before. Issie and I were talking last week about having more kids and how children ought to have siblings so that they aren't alone in the world. I left you alone, Teddi. I'd expect better from my son, and I expect better from me."

I am speechless. David says again that he's going to straighten out my mother, and I reach out and catch his sleeve before he can. "You can tell her about Isolde," I say, "but don't tell her about the rest, okay?"

"You're too good to her," he tells me.

"Maybe," I say. She is a royal pain. Still, I know what happened to her and I don't know who I'd be if it had happened to me. "Cody is a delicious little boy," I say.

The cloud that passes over David's face is so dark I'm almost sorry I said it. Who would have thought that losing his son the way my mother did, especially when he lives beside the water, hadn't ever occurred to him? "Still," he says, recovering, "Markie died over thirty years ago. You let her off the hook too easily."

"It's a deep hook."

There's a squeal of delight from downstairs, followed by Isolde's lilting voice shouting up the stairs that dinner is ready.

David looks toward my mother's room, but the pull of his wife's voice is too strong and we go down the stairs together.

Near the head of the table, where my father is seated, my grandmother's menorah rests in the place of honor. Issie has made it shine, and everyone agrees that she should have the honor of lighting the candles. Okay, everyone but Alyssa, who has to be reminded of how she got burned after insisting she could light the candles.

Issie says that she's never lit a menorah before. With my father's quick intake of breath she quickly amends her statement, adding that David has always done it in their home. She tells Alyssa she could use her help.

Alyssa instructs her in the napkin-on-the-head tradition and Issie looks skeptical. Dana and I don the napkin hats and, with a look to David for confirmation, she joins us. As she lights the candles, we sing the prayer, more quietly than usual because there are new ears to hear our pathetic voices.

When the eighth candle is lit, I do the hand thing, circling the candles and gathering the smoke before closing my eyes and putting my hands over my face. Everyone knows what I am thankful for, and if they don't, Cody, happily ensconced in his father's arms, squeaks up to remind them.

I pick up the menorah and carefully put it on the windowsill so the world can see our faith. I make sure the base is steady and as I touch it I make my last Chanukah wish of the year.

That we can all be together again.

My mother appears in the doorway. I think about the wish I just made and remind myself that I did say *all*.

"What aren't you telling me?" she says, her eyes darting about and landing on Cody. She gasps and leans against the doorway.

David opens his mouth, but my father steals the show. He

points with his fork and announces with great authority, "Issie is David's wife. This is their son. Sit down. We're eating."

My mother is nonplussed.

"No birth announcement?" she says. "No wedding? Your phone is broken?"

My father interrupts what will clearly be a diatribe. "We are having a meal here. A celebratory meal. I have a second grandson. I have a new daughter-in-law. You can choose to celebrate that, or you can go upstairs and have bupkas."

Issie looks confused so David translates for her. "Nothing," he says. "Bupkas is nothing."

My mother clutches her chest. "This is how you dress a child in New York in the winter?" she asks, staring at Cody's dark curly hair and chocolate skin peeking out from his thin, stretchy all-in-one. "We'll call Bloomingdale's tomorrow."

Drew goes into the kitchen and returns with an extra chair. My mother points at it to indicate he can take the kitchen chair and she will sit on one of the new ones. Like everyone else in my family, Drew obeys.

"They make high chairs to match this set?" my mother asks me.

I tell her I'll check into it in the morning, and take Cody from David so that he can pass the platter of latkes that Howard has helped Issie prepare.

My mother looks at me. Pointedly she looks at Howard and back at me. She looks at Drew and back at me. "If they make the high chairs," she starts.

"No," I tell her, trying to head her off at the pass. "Don't even—"

"What?" she asks innocently.

We are all silent. All waiting.

"Just if they do, you should maybe get two."

I bury my head behind the baby while Drew and Howard stare at the ceiling and my brother, David, laughs.

* * * * *

THE PERFECT CHRISTMAS

MARY SCHRAMSKI

CHAPTER 1

December 22

"Gwen?"

"Hi, Mom," I say into my cell phone. "How are you?" It's 6:00 a.m. and I'm driving to the office.

"I'm fine. I was just wondering…how about coming home for Christmas?"

My mother's request surprises me. We haven't spent a Christmas together in seven years. "I was planning on working."

"I just thought it would be nice to have you home for the holiday."

"I'd love to be there, but I'm on a big health insurance case." I take a deep breath, watch the road. A few moments ago, before my mother called, it started snowing. I know she will understand that I have to work, can't come home. She was an emergency room doctor before she retired six months ago and for years she worked fourteen hours a day.

"You can't take just a few days off?" she asks.

My eyes open wider with her request. This doesn't sound

like my mother at all. "I thought you might be able to come down tonight, stay till the morning of the twenty-sixth. Nobody works on Christmas, Gwen."

"Yes, people do, like you, remember?" Instead of laughing and saying she remembers when she used to be at the hospital all the time, she sighs. And my mother is not the type of woman who sighs.

"Mom, are you okay?"

"I'm fine. Just disappointed. I was so hoping I'd get to see you for the holiday."

"I wish I could come home. I'm really sorry. Can I call you back when I get to the office? I'm on the freeway." I ask, feel more uneasiness.

"You don't have to. I know you're busy. I'll talk to you later." And she's gone.

The last thing on my mind this morning is celebrating Christmas. I'm up to my ears in legal briefs. I know it's not emergency room work—saving lives at a moment's notice, like my mother did—but being a good attorney is important to me. Maybe my mother is lonely. And that *sigh?* She's always been in charge of her feelings, her life, and the ER, where she was chief physician for the last fifteen years. She's a woman who fixes things—like broken arms and gunshot wounds, heart attacks, and kitchen sinks when they back up.

Guilt begins to fill my chest, mixes with the worry that is already there. It's pretty pathetic for a forty-year-old to feel guilty about not going home for Christmas. I put my cell phone on the passenger seat then turn my attention back to the expressway. I take the familiar exit, weave slowly through the deserted Boston streets to my office, slip into my reserved parking space and turn off the car. It's so quiet I can hear the soft whisper of snowflakes falling against the windshield.

Snow.

When I was a kid in Florida, I used to dream of snowy Christmases. My mother raised me by herself in Boca Raton, and every Christmas till junior high, I would close my eyes and wish for a snowstorm to hit Florida, so big that the hospital would close and my mother would stay home. Of course the snowstorm never happened, and she spent most of the holidays at the hospital.

I glance at my cell and think about her sighing a few minutes ago. Something's not right. And even though I tell myself not to, I'm worried.

"You're here," my mother says, then hugs me. A moment ago I found her waiting for me in the baggage claim of the West Palm Beach Airport.

"Yes, I'm here." I smile, wrap my arms around her then let go, step back. She looks healthy, even happy, and I wonder if I made the right decision to come here. This morning, right after I walked into my office, more worry filled my chest. I tried to tell myself it was silly, but I couldn't get the sound of my mother's sigh out of my mind. So at ten o'clock I called

American Airlines, made a reservation to fly to Florida for three days. Then I packed my laptop, stuffed my briefcase, talked to my assistant and after I cleaned off my desk, drove back home to pack. I made the flight to West Palm Beach with only five minutes to spare.

"I'm so glad to see you," she says.

"I'm glad to see you, too. I have a ton of work to do, though." I hold up my briefcase.

"That's fine. We'll fit your work in around some fun. It's just nice to have you home."

"Thanks." People say we look alike and I agree. We are both tall, blond and slender. "Why was it so important I come home?"

She looks directly into my eyes and laughs. "It's…Christmas, did you forget?"

"Mother, you know me. I could care less about Christmas and I thought you felt the same way."

She smiles. "Maybe this year you'll change your mind. I have. And I've got some great holiday things planned for us."

"Really?" I laugh, expect her to laugh, too, but she doesn't. She *sighs* again.

"Did you check a bag?" She looks at my roller bag that I'm so used to traveling with.

"This is it for three days. I didn't think I'd need much—shorts, T-shirts, jeans."

She stares at me again, presses her lips together and looks concerned. "You look tired, Gwen."

"I'm fine. Of course, I'm working too hard. I'm trying to make partner this year. If anyone should understand working too hard, it's you."

I laugh and a moment later so does she, but there is something in her gaze that makes me wonder if she thinks what I've said is really funny.

"Well, thank you for taking the time from your busy schedule to come home. You can relax for a few days, get some rest. It'll be just the two of us, and Janie on Christmas Day, like it used to be." She takes my arm then turns her head a little, looks so serious it makes my heart beat a little faster. "Like I said, I've planned a few Christmas activities for us to do. I hope you don't mind."

"Like what?"

"You'll see," she says and leads the way out of the airport.

We arrived at the house a few minutes ago. My mother has lived in the same modest house since I was eight years old. It's on a quiet residential street in Boca Raton, with a small, lush front yard filled with hibiscuses and one lone palm tree. The backyard has more flowers and a large patch of grass. In the seven years since I've been away, I forgot how green everything is in Florida in the winter, and how warm it is compared to Boston.

I'm exhausted even though it's only nine-thirty. When we walked in the house from the garage, I cut across the kitchen, trudged down the hall and found the guest room. Then I opened my suitcase, changed into pajamas and made my way to the living room.

My mother is sitting at the end of the couch, staring out the window into the dark front yard. The only light in the room is coming from the kitchen. In the dim light she looks younger, like the young woman I remember when I was little. Many times, after she came home from the hospital, I'd wake, pad into the living room and find her sitting right where she is now with that same solemn expression.

"Mother," I say quietly.

She turns and smiles. "Do you need anything?"

I move to the couch. She's still dressed in her lightweight blue sweater and functional khaki pants. The window above the brown leather couch is open and a warm breeze floats in, covers us. I think about the Boston snow I left this afternoon and for some reason I shiver. More tropical air envelops us, takes the memory away and I sit at the opposite end of the couch and yawn.

"Excuse me," I say.

"You're tired."

"I am. Probably from traveling. But the night before last I was up till 1:00 a.m. working on the health insurance case I told you about." I nod toward the guest room where my briefcase is.

Through the dim light she studies me for a moment. "I know your work is important, but sometimes you have to stop and smell the roses. You know, try to find a happy medium between work and other things."

I raise an eyebrow. "Like you ever did? You never would have become head of the emergency room if you stopped to smell *anything*."

"True. I worked hard for so many years." She nods, then turns her attention back to the window. The house is quiet except for the usual noises, creaks and groans of the house, crickets chirping. Outside someone starts a car. "Sometimes I think I worked too hard," she says.

"You did do that." And then there's silence between us.

"So it's almost Christmas," I say to fill up the space. A memory floats in—me waiting up for my mother on Christmas Eve, on this same couch, hoping there would be no emergencies on Christmas Day so she could stay home and enjoy dinner, open gifts with me.

"I have a big day planned for us tomorrow," she says, looking at me. "I want this to be your best Christmas ever."

"*Best Christmas ever?* That doesn't sound like you. We've never made a big deal out of Christmas."

"We always had a tree." She nods toward the corner of the living room where Janie, our housekeeper, and I would put up the artificial tree a week before Christmas.

"True, we did have a tree. But that was about it."

"And there were always presents." Mother shifts, crosses her arms.

"Yes, that's true." I don't say what else I'm thinking. That Janie did all of my mother's Christmas shopping, and she would watch me open my gifts when my mother got called to the hospital on an emergency, which was most of the time. Holidays always brought lots of falls, burns, heart attacks, drunk drivers.

"I was going to buy a Christmas tree yesterday, but then I thought you might like to help pick it out. And I wanted to make sure you could come home. We can shop tomorrow afternoon for decorations, and decorate the tree tomorrow night while we listen to music and drink hot chocolate. And there's a Christmas program at the city park that I thought you might like. Then on Christmas Eve we can attend church. I've already checked on service times. And Christmas Day we'll have a traditional turkey dinner." She smiles.

"Wow," I whisper. I study her to see if she's kidding. She's not. "Who's going to cook Christmas dinner? Didn't Janie retire when you did?"

"I thought you and I could. Anyone can cook if they can read. I also thought we could make Christmas cookies. We've never done that before."

"No, we haven't, but we've never jumped off the roof together, either, Mom. You do realize I'm not much of a cook?"

She shakes her head, laughs. "Well, I'm not, either, but I thought we could give it a try." She turns and stares out the window again. "That'll be part of the fun of this holiday." Her tone is so wistful.

I touch her shoulder. "Are you okay?" I wait for her to turn back to me but she doesn't. "You seem different. You've never really been into Christmas before and now all these activities. Why the change?"

Finally she turns back. "I just want this to be a nice Christmas for you, that's all. It's been so long since you've been home for the holidays, and I never had a lot of time when I was practicing."

I press my lips together. "You know, if all these plans are for me, I don't mind if we don't do anything. I have so much work to do, we don't have to do any of that crazy Christmas stuff. I don't even like Christmas, really."

She shakes her head. "No, they're for me, too." Then she looks at me quizzically. "You really don't like Christmas?"

"Not really."

"Why not?"

"Because…I guess…maybe because it's all hype and a lot of extra work."

"But I thought this year we could do some fun things. When I was working Christmas, the hospital would get so busy. But now…I'm home."

"Mother, you always used to tell me that Christmas was too commercial."

She nods. "Yes, I remember. But I've come to realize it doesn't have to be. It can be fun if it's planned right. A holiday can be wonderful if planned correctly."

"Your plans sound pretty ambitious." I shift my attention toward the guest room then back to her.

"I think I made you too serious. You need to relax more, Gwen."

A tiny kernel of unfamiliar frustration begins to pulse in my stomach and surprises me, but I manage to push it back. "I'll try, but I do have a few things to finish while I'm here."

She raises her eyebrow. "I know your work's important. I was just hoping you could take a few days off and enjoy our time together. How about that?"

She seems so worried, so different from what I'm used to, I really don't know how to answer her.

CHAPTER 2

December 23

I've been working on my laptop since 5:00 a.m. Now it's eight-thirty. When I woke up this morning, I tiptoed to the bathroom, quietly came back to the guest room and gritted my teeth against the strong urge I had for coffee. I didn't want to wake my mother so I turned on the light over the desk in the corner and began working. My mother was always an early riser when I lived at home, but now that she's retired I'm assuming she sleeps in.

"Gwen, dear," Mother whispers through my closed bedroom door.

"I'm up," I say, turn off my laptop and begin straightening my notes in the corner of the desk. I did make some progress on the briefs this morning.

She opens the door and the aroma of coffee wafts in. I close my eyes, sniff. "That coffee smells so good. I was working." I gesture to my computer.

She glances at the desk. "Did you get a lot done?"

"I did. I got up early. The house was so quiet. I figured you sleep late now."

She smiles. "Sometimes I do. Come on, I'll get you a cup of coffee." She waves me toward her. I follow her down the hall into the bright Florida kitchen. It looks the same as I remember—the way Janie decorated it years ago—light yellow walls, not much on the counters, a large window by the breakfast table that faces the backyard.

"I heard on the news there was a big snowstorm in Boston last night," she says. "It's lucky you decided to come here when you did." She pours coffee in a tan mug. "Just think if you hadn't left when you did, you'd be all alone in Boston for Christmas."

"Yes," I say, think about my quiet house, with its quiet office, where I sometimes work all night. She hands me my coffee. I take a sip and groan with satisfaction.

"You should have made coffee right when you got up." She crosses the kitchen.

"I wasn't sure how late you sleep so I didn't want to wake you. I know with retirement your schedule's probably changed a little."

My mother fills another tan mug then sits across from me at the pine kitchen table. "It has. I do sleep in a bit, but not much. I'm usually up around seven. But this morning I actually woke at five-forty-five. I was so excited about your being here. I stayed in bed because I didn't want to wake you."

We both laugh.

"Here we were, both awake, me lying in bed, you dying for a cup of coffee, waiting for the other to get up." She smiles. "Not knowing what the other was thinking."

"It's okay. The work I accomplished was worth the suffering."

"I'm glad you got some things done. Now we can enjoy ourselves today." She studies me for a moment. "Gwen, are you dating anyone special?"

I pull back a little. "Well, that's completely out of left field. We don't usually talk about my social life."

"I was just wondering."

"Not right now. I don't have the time." I leave out the part that ever since I broke up with Aaron I just don't have the guts to get involved with anyone. For months he forgot to tell me he found someone else. His excuse was I was working too much.

"Don't wait too long to find someone. Time can get away from you," Mother says.

I take a deep breath, brush back the memory of Aaron.

"I'm really married to my work right now."

"Remember how I used to bring tons of paperwork home from the hospital?"

"How could I forget?" My mother was always working. At times when I was young I just wanted to shake her and tell her to stay home. But as I got older, I guess I got used to it.

"That part of my life is over now." In the bright morning sunlight she looks older than I remember. And there is a nervousness in her eyes I've never seen before. "All that work I did. At times I thought it would bury me. And then when I retired, poof, it's over and there's no definite place to be. It's a little scary, really." She stands, goes to the coffee pot and adds coffee to her mug. "You want more?"

"No, I'm fine." I raise the cup to my lips, take a sip. Then it hits me. Maybe she's feeling at loose ends because she's retired, and that's why she was so insistent about my coming home. It has to be difficult for a woman who was so busy to just stop working.

"Mother?"

"Yes?" She glances up, walks over to the table and sits back down.

"Are you happy with retirement? You seem a little nervous, a little…I don't know, maybe not like yourself."

She bites her bottom lip then smiles this big smile that is really not like her at all. "Of course I'm fine. The retirement took some time getting used to, you know, not being at the hospital all the time, but I volunteer and read. I've had time to think about things, clean out my files, the garage."

I nod, but I'm not sure that she's as *fine* as she wants me to believe. "Volunteering is a good way to spend your free time."

"Speaking of time, we should get going." She stands. "Why don't you have breakfast, then we'll get on the road?" She goes to the sink and dumps out her coffee and pulls out a cereal box from the upper right-hand cabinet. "There's milk in the fridge, bananas—" she holds up a bunch and wiggles them at me "—You have to get your potassium, you know."

"Yes, I remember." I stand, find a bowl and pour some Raisin Bran in it, peel a banana and slice it on top of the cereal. "About all these Christmas plans?" I say.

"What about them?"

I go to the refrigerator, find the milk and see a huge turkey on the bottom shelf. Oh, God. I close the door and go back to the counter by the sink.

"We don't have to do so much. I'd like to relax, maybe go out for a nice dinner on Christmas Day and leave it at that. Then you can rest and I'll work on the briefs that are due the first of the year."

She frowns. "I don't need to rest! And are you in that big of a rush with your work?"

"Well, yes and no. I have a generous time frame, but I want them perfect." I've been told I'm a workaholic and I know I work at some things too hard—but that's how I've gotten this far.

"You always seem to do well," she says.

"I know. I just thought we could have fun hanging out." I'm hoping what I've just said might make her relax a little but her expression turns to sheer disappointment. And this really bothers me. Before I went off to Princeton, we lived a peaceful—yet distant—life, she working and me trying to do well in school. My mother always encouraged me, but it was a passing smile, a pat on the shoulder after she'd looked at my report card or before she walked out the door. We didn't intersect a lot because she was so busy. And when I got to high school I was busy, too. But there were never any fights, disagreements.

"So you just want to hang out? But I made all these plans," she says. "I don't want to just hang out and not do some Christmas activities. I want to celebrate Christmas! We need to do that. It's only for a few days, and then you can go back to Boston and work hard. You know, I found from working forty-some years, that work worries aren't all that important."

To my surprise, aggravation begins to fill my chest. "Work isn't important when you're retired!"

"But worrying doesn't make anything better. And you've always done a good job."

"I was planning on using some of my time here to polish some things. When I'm home the office phone rings constantly—"

The phone rings and I raise my eyebrow at the coincidence. My mother crosses the kitchen, picks up the receiver.

"Hi, Janie." She nods, smiles at me. "Yes, she made it here on time."

Janie began working for my mother when she was nineteen, after she divorced her husband. She never remarried, never had any children of her own and she was a great housekeeper.

"You're coming over Christmas Day, right?" My mother again smiles. "Good, well, come over early, I have lots of things planned. And don't bring anything. Gwen and I will do all the cooking."

I wince. Neither one of us has any practice cooking Christmas dinner.

"Yes, we have a lot to do these next two days." She says goodbye and walks back to where I'm standing. "Now where were we?"

"Mother, this is so strange. I can't remember one time you made a big deal out of any holiday, especially Christmas, and now…what's going on?"

"A few days ago I was going through some boxes in the garage and I realized how much I missed celebrating Christmas when I was working. So I started making a list. Christmas is really a happy holiday."

I laugh. "Happy? Most people get depressed around this time. I think…" I stop because more disappointment begins to grow in her gaze.

"You think what?" she asks.

Suddenly my mother is sniffing back tears. My doctor-mother, the one who looks at everything so analytically, the one who has always been so strong, I think is crying.

"Are you crying?"

"It's nothing." She finds a white paper napkin on the counter, dabs at her eyes. "Nothing at all. It must be my hormones."

"Is something wrong with your hormones?" I take a step toward her, but she holds up her hand and I stop.

"Of course not. I keep a close tab on them." But her voice is husky with tears.

"Well, then it couldn't be that. What's wrong?"

"Maybe it's the season that's getting to me, making me blue."

"See, I told you, Christmas is depressing." I move next to her, pat her shoulder. "Christmas has never gotten to you before when we didn't do anything."

"No, it's not Christmas. I'm happy about it"

"Then what is it?"

"I...don't know. I made these plans and was so hoping..." she looks at me, sniffs, then walks over to the recipe desk where Janie used to pay all the bills and plan our meals. She picks up a piece of paper and takes a deep breath. "But right now...I'd be happy if we could do just a few things on my list."

I cross the kitchen, gently take the paper from her and read it. It's written in my mother's almost illegible doctor's handwriting:

Christmas Shopping
Get tree and decorations
Groceries
Caroling
Church
Christmas Dinner

"Caroling?" I ask, pointing to the word. "We've never done any of these things together except maybe grocery shop."

She shrugs. "That's the point. I thought they might be fun

for us to do. I read about a caroling group that's going to meet in the town center tomorrow night."

"It's going to be eighty degrees today, seventy-five tonight. I'm not sure I feel much like caroling in a heat wave." I stare, try to figure out what's going on with her.

"Well, we don't have to do that one." She looks at the list again. "But my heart is really set on all these other things." She points to her list then sniffs again. "The other night when I couldn't sleep, I made the list and I thought these would make the perfect Christmas."

"You couldn't sleep? Was something bothering you?"

She looks at me for a moment. "No, it was warm, I'd been cleaning out the garage and I was overly tired. Anyway, these will make the perfect Christmas."

"I learned a long time ago there's no perfect anything," I say and then I'm sorry because her expression changes to defeat. Even though my mother and I aren't close, I do love her and would never want to hurt her or make her cry. "Okay, wait a minute," I say.

"What?"

"Let's do some things this morning and see how it goes. Then we'll regroup after lunch, and I can get some work done."

She claps her hands like a child. "That's such a good idea. You'll see, you're going to have a great time."

"I think we should get a big tree," my mother says as she pulls her Nissan into the packed Wal-Mart parking lot.

"A big tree? Really?"

"Yes, one that will reach to the top of the living room ceiling." She pats the top of her head.

"How are we going to get it home?"

Mom slips the car into one of the last parking spaces, turns the ignition off and looks over at me. "We're going to tie it on the top of the car and drive home. That's what I've seen other people do."

"We could just get a small tree. One that would fit in the trunk. Remember Janie always did a small artificial tree because it was easy to store. It looked just fine in the corner. What happened to it?"

"I threw it away a few years ago. A bigger tree will be wonderful—more festive. We need to make the house smell like Christmas and buy new decorations, too."

"You threw the tree away?" To my surprise, my stomach sinks a little.

She nods. "I didn't think I'd need it."

"What happened to the decorations we had?"

She leans back, looks at me. "I threw them out along with the tree." She sighs, the same sad sigh I'm still not used to hearing, the one that brought me here.

"I was trying to make room for some medical books and files…."

"Oh, Mom, don't worry about it. Why would you think you'd need them? Maybe you just got distracted," I say, trying to make her feel better and me, too. But I feel sad that the decorations from my childhood are gone. "We had those decorations for a long time."

"I know. It was stupid."

I take a deep breath, realize sitting in the car feeling badly about Christmas decorations isn't going to solve anything. "Oh, well, we can get more decorations. We'll get better decorations!"

She smiles at me. "Maybe we should buy the decorations first and then the tree after." She opens her car door, climbs out and so do I. The short horn honk tells me she's locked the car.

"I thought after we get the tree and set it up, we could go do the grocery shopping for our Christmas dinner, and…" She sounds out of breath, a little stressed.

I walk around the car. "Mother, it's fine. We'll just take one step at a time. Neither one of us has much experience with spearheading Christmas. Plus, you have the turkey already. I saw it in the fridge. That's one thing you can check off your list."

With the Florida sun shining in her eyes, she squints at me. A warm, gentle breeze surrounds us. It certainly doesn't feel like Christmas—more like July. I look over to the Christmas trees in the far left corner of the parking lot. There are very few left. "Rudolph the Red-Nosed Reindeer" begins to play from the loudspeakers on the Wal-Mart roof and for some reason I feel irritated.

"You have more experience with Christmas than I have," she says.

"What?"

My mother visors her eyes with her right hand, and I realize we are the same height. For some weird reason I always thought my mother was taller than me.

"Janie took care of Christmas, the tree, dinner and did the shopping. You helped her, so you have all this experience."

I nod. "Sure. When I was little we used to decorate the tree, wrap presents, bake cookies."

A tiny memory rushes in. Janie and me in the kitchen cutting out Christmas cookies, setting up red and green frosting bowls on the kitchen counter, and me wishing my mother could be with us.

"When I was a kid, we didn't do anything for Christmas," she says, brings me back to the Wal-Mart parking lot. "My father was always working."

I lean against my mother's Nissan, look at her. My maternal grandmother passed away when my mother was only five, but I've rarely thought of what it was like for my mom around the holidays. "So your father didn't decorate, make plans for you and your brothers and sisters? I always imagined your home life filled with people and laughter."

She studies the clear sky. "Oh, no. Dad was so busy trying to feed us, I don't think he knew it *was* Christmas." Her attention shifts to the behemoth Wal-Mart. "You think we should buy the decorations before we buy the tree?"

"Definitely. That way we can tie the tree to the roof of the car and go directly home."

She smiles. "Good idea."

We trudge across the crowded parking lot to the Wal-Mart, go through the automatic doors. "I'll Be Home For Christmas" is playing loudly, and the store is packed with people.

"It looks like we aren't the only ones who thought of shopping this morning," I say.

"I think the crowds make it seem more like Christmas, more festive, don't you think?"

"More like torture," I whisper.

"Christmas decorations?" Mother asks the woman in the red Santa hat and vest who's standing by a small group of shopping carts.

"Aisle four. But there's not much left." The woman pushes a shopping cart toward my mother. "Merry Christmas."

"Thank you," Mother says, smiling again.

Aisle four looks like a nuclear winter has taken place. The shelves are nearly empty and boxes and paper are strewn on the floor.

"Okay. So we're still buying a big tree?" I ask.

She nods. "Yes, I think that would be best."

"How many ornaments and lights do we need?"

"I have no idea." Mother looks around as if she's lost.

"You know, we could just get one of those fake trees." I point to two bedraggled boxes across the aisle that I spied when we turned the corner. "That way we wouldn't have to buy lights, and you'd have it for next year."

She shakes her head. "No. We need a real tree, with real

lights. A fake one won't smell like a real one. Come on, we're both smart women, we can figure out how many lights and ornaments we have to have."

"But here's some pine scent." I hold up the only can of pine room spray left, shake it. "A fake tree can smell like a real one."

"No." She looks down the aisle. "There's certainly not much left. The news said last night that holiday spending was down. I just assumed that we'd have a good pick of items."

"If we buy a big tree, we probably will need a foot of lights for each foot so that's at least sixty feet of lights, right?" I ask.

"Yes, that's correct. And if we put ten ornaments per foot we need sixty ornaments?"

"Okay, lights first." I walk down the aisle, find the place where the lights *should* be. The only ones left are four boxes of chilli pepper lights. There are no white lights, no fat red or blue ones, either. I loved the tiny white lights that Janie used to wind around the artificial tree. I'd stare at them on Christmas Eve, usually when I was waiting for my mother to come home. I push the boxes around, bend down and look for more, but there aren't any.

"They don't have white lights," I say, looking at my mom, who is standing in front of the ornaments about three feet from me.

"What, dear?"

"They don't have white lights. Just these stupid looking chilli pepper things." To my surprise my chest has begun to hurt a little.

"And you had your heart set on white lights?" She looks up, frowns.

"Well, no, not set. It's just what I'm used to. Janie always used white lights and I loved them."

She closes the space between us, checks the shelf, picks up a box of the plastic red chillies strung on dark green electrical cord and makes a face. "Good God. We'll have to go somewhere else."

"Where in the world can we go? If Wal-Mart is sold out, every other place must be sold out, too. Plus we don't have a lot of time," I say.

"But if you had your heart set on white lights…I want everything just right."

Her tone is so sad I put my hand on her shoulder. "It's okay, Mom, really." Then I look at my watch. It's already eleven. "I don't know why we have to have a tree, anyway. It's just us. Janie will be over on Christmas Day but—"

"This is so awful." She rubs her forehead with her fingertips.

"It's not that awful." Her reaction is definitely not like her. She's never worried about small things like tree lights or Christmas stock at Wal-Mart.

"There's really nothing here."

"Actually, you know what? I think something different might be fun," I say, putting the box of chilli lights in the cart. "These are unique. Let's get them."

"Fun? You think these might be fun?" She shakes another box at me. "Really?"

"Yes. Our lives have changed. You're retired and I'm an attorney ready to make partner. Chilli pepper Christmas lights are just what we need." I tell the small white lie to make her feel better.

"Okay." My mother stacks another box in the cart, then moves over to the ornaments. "This section is as bare as the others."

I glance up and down the aisle. We are the only two shoppers in this area. I guess everyone got an early start this year except us.

"There's only pink." She points to the numerous boxes of huge pink balls.

I count the boxes silently. "At least there are enough."

"But…when you were little what did you want?"

I turn to her, smile a little. "That was such a long time ago. I wish you wouldn't worry so much."

"I know. But I want everything to be nice."

"Let's just get what they have and make the best of it." I step toward the ornaments, pick up a box.

She picks up another box and stares at them.

"Pink Christmas ornaments and red chillies. I don't know," I say. "We might start a new trend, a tradition. At least it will be different." I leave out that I'm not sure how this combination is going to look.

"You think so?" She takes a step toward me.

I shrug. "Maybe. We can try."

"We could look for other ornaments somewhere else."

I glance at my watch again. "Mom, it's after eleven on December 23. If Wal-Mart doesn't have what we're looking for, nobody else is going to have anything better. You're making way too much of this."

She places her hand on my shoulder and I can feel her body heat through my T-shirt. "I want things nice this year because when you were little I was so busy."

"Well, you know what I really wanted when I was little? What I really wanted was for us to decorate a tree together. I'm not sure I cared what it looked like. I did want lots of tinsel, though, and you home for the holiday. And that's what I have now, so what could be better?"

To my surprise a lump begins to form in my throat. That was all I ever wanted—my mother home, and us working together to make Christmas like I saw on TV. I heard stories from other kids at school, how their mothers and fathers decorated the tree together, how they spent time at their grandparents' house, too. I was always so jealous.

"But pink ornaments and chillies?" She shakes the ornament box and stares at me as if she needs reassurance.

"Let's try it."

"Then we need to get tinsel. I saw it around here somewhere." She walks down the aisle, picks up six boxes of tinsel. "We have tinsel! We can decorate the tree tonight."

"Good. Then we can get out of here and go get the tree." I start piling boxes of ornaments in the cart on top of the red chillies. The checkout line is going to be at least another thirty minutes, then we've got to go buy the tree and groceries. That will put us at late afternoon before we even start to decorate. "Have Yourself A Merry Little Christmas" begins to play over the loudspeaker. I shake my head and wonder if that is even possible.

CHAPTER 3

We finally made it home.

After we stood in the Wal-mart checkout line for forty-five minutes, we drove across the parking lot to buy a Christmas tree. Mom took thirty minutes to decide on the best tree, which was, I have to admit, difficult because the leftover trees were pretty scraggly. She finally decided on a five-foot-high, terribly dehydrated Douglas fir. Now I'm afraid if a heat source comes within ten feet of the tree it's going to ignite.

After we bought the tree and the man tied it to the top of the car, we both realized at the same time that we didn't have a Christmas tree holder so I ran back into Wal-Mart to find one. It took another thirty minutes to get through the checkout line, and the whole time I imagined the tree, strapped to the top of my mother's blue Nissan in the warm Florida sunshine, losing a handful of needles with every ring of the cash register.

Once we got home, my mother and I struggled to untie the tree from the car. Her neighbor, Mr. D'Angelo, came over and helped us haul it off the top of the car and into the house.

He also helped us set it in the tree holder, in the corner where Janie's neat little tree always stood. The tree is lanky and a lot of needles fell off when we dragged it through the living room. I picked up most of them then got out the vacuum and cleaned up the rest. Now the tree's in place and my mother is staring at it as if a miracle has appeared in her living room.

"It's really quite nice, don't you think?" she asks as I cross the living room and sit on the couch.

I study the tree. It's leaning to the left, but our neighbor said that's the best he could do. "It's a little crooked don't you think?" I ask then wish I hadn't said anything.

My mother frowns and tilts her head a bit. "I think I can fix it if you'll help me."

"How?"

She walks into the kitchen and comes back with a book. "If you'll push the tree a little, I'll just prop it up, then it'll sit straight."

I get up, go to the tree and tilt it to the right. "Like this?" More needles fall to the floor.

"Yes, I'll put this under it." She bends down and shoves the thin book under the metal holder, then stands, and we take a few steps back and look. "That did it. It looks pretty good now, don't you think?" she asks.

"If we could just fix the dryness it would look better. Does it look bald in some places?" As I say this, I see worry overtaking expression. A few years ago she would have agreed, thrown her hands up and said she had to get back to work.

"Is it that bad?"

"It's okay, Mom, but you have to admit it's a little dry. Maybe once it sucks up some of that water it'll be better. And after we get the lights and ornaments on, it will be just fine."

"You think you'll like it?"

"It's just a tree. You're worrying too much."

She sits at the end of the couch, crosses her arms. "I know. I just wanted everything this year to be nice. I guess I should have started earlier, but I wasn't sure you could come home, and I wanted us to do all this together but…"

"But what?"

"It's just not turning out the way I planned." She nods toward the Christmas tree then looks at me and purses her lips.

"Does anything turn out the way it's planned? The tree will be just fine once we get it decorated," I say, but realize only a miracle is going to make that tree look better.

"There aren't enough lights," Mom says, then plugs in the last strand.

The chilli pepper lights actually don't look as bad as I thought they were going to. The red next to the green tree adds a nice holiday touch. However, my mother is right. All the strands only reach to the middle of the tree. Somehow we calculated incorrectly.

"Do you think we should try to find more lights?" she asks, stepping back and I do, too.

"More chilli peppers? Where in the world would we find them?"

"I don't know."

"The tree looks…okay, really." I was going to say the tree looks fine, but I can't tell that big of a lie to anyone, especially my mother. "Maybe we can spread them out with extension cords."

"That's a good idea."

We both take another step back. Then as if on cue, we look at each other and laugh.

"It's awful," she says.

"No, it's okay."

"I guess we should put the ornaments on, then go grocery shopping?"

I check my watch. It's already three-thirty. Tonight the stores will probably be packed with last-minute grocery shoppers and there's nothing I hate more than a crowded grocery store. And tomorrow it's going to be worse. This afternoon I had planned on working, and I was also hoping to get some more work done tonight.

"Let's go to the store now, come back, and then decorate the tree. Then after supper I can work. Do we need to make a list?" I ask.

"No, I made one a few days ago. I thought we'd have the traditional dinner—turkey, mashed potatoes, gravy, cranberry sauce, a salad." My mother straightens, stares at the tree.

"That sounds great," I say, crossing my arms, and wondering how we are ever going to get it all fixed.

"You know, your time here is so short, if you want I can go to the store. That way you can work a little. But we still need to put the balls and tinsel on tonight," she says, nodding toward the tree.

"Well, if that's okay with you. That way I can get some work done while you're gone."

"When I come back I'll make some hot chocolate, and we can play Christmas music while we work on the tree." The expression in her eyes is so…I'm not even sure how to describe it, maybe desperate, and this reaction isn't like my mother at all.

"Mom, you seem so agitated."

"What do you mean?" Her hand goes to her chest. "I'm just fine. I'm worried about you. Do you think you might be working too hard?"

I laugh, shake my head. "It's not a question of *might*. I am, but that's what I have to do to make partner. You should understand that part of my life." I point to the tree. "I'm worried about you, too. And, you know…well, all this. What's it all for? Christmas doesn't mean anything to me."

She seems shocked at what I've just said. "That's not true. I'd better go to the grocery store." She crosses the room, walks to the kitchen.

I follow her as a tiny, unfamiliar storm brews in my chest. "Mother? You seem upset at what I said. Are you?"

"No, I'm not." She turns with her grocery list in hand.

"You sure look upset. I was just telling you how I feel."

She bites her bottom lip, crosses her arms. "Well, to be honest, I just don't want you to make the same mistakes I did."

"What mistakes? What are you talking about?"

She walks over to the dishwasher, begins putting our clean breakfast dishes away—cereal bowls on the second shelf, glasses on the bottom one. When the dishes are all where they should be, she turns to me, her lips flat against each other.

"Maybe it's my fault you're so cynical, Gwen."

"Me, cynical? I'm not."

"You just said Christmas doesn't mean anything to you. That's pretty cynical, don't you think?"

A memory slides in, one of my mother in scrubs, standing in the kitchen by the dishwasher, ready to go to the hospital on Christmas morning and me, hoping she wouldn't go. She was waiting for Janie, and I held her hand, not wanting to let go. I never told her I didn't want her to go. She had explained so many times that she helped people, saved lives—how could I ask her not to do that?

"I do think you're a bit cynical," she says again.

"It's just, well, I got used to not celebrating when I was a kid. Habits die hard, you know." I immediately regret my harsh tone, but I feel so frustrated. "I mean, I never thought you liked Christmas, either."

"I certainly didn't hate it."

"But it always seemed like such an imposition for you." And to my surprise, my throat tightens.

"Is that how you remember me at Christmas?"

"Yes, that's what I remember." Another small, angry storm begins to swirl in my chest. "That was your busiest time at the hospital, and I felt like I was standing in your way."

"I did my best." She crosses her arms. "I had to work, and the holidays were always busy at the hospital."

"But you always…you put your job before me." My voice cracks with hurt.

"Well…everyone makes mistakes, and I'm sorry. I just don't want you to do the same thing." And then she turns and walks out the door to the garage. I hear the large garage door open, the car start.

A moment later I realize how quiet the house is without anyone here. I used to stand right here on Christmas Eve, think how soundless the house was. I must have been in high school. Mom was at the hospital and I'd think about my father and wonder what it would be like to know him, have parents home for Christmas, maybe brothers and sisters, like my mother did.

My heart begins to hurt with the memory. I go to the sink, fill a glass with water, drink and push the memory away. Then I walk back into the living room and look at the Christmas tree.

The tree still looks dumb. I should go to the guest room, turn on my laptop and begin working, but at the moment I can't. Did my mother and I just have a fight? I'm not sure because we've never really fought. I sit on the couch, stare at the tree. The late Florida sunshine is blazing through the large picture window and makes the tree look more ridiculous.

I love my mother, but she's acting so different than what I'm used to. And with all this Christmas stuff she's planned, it's obvious she doesn't know me very well. I get up, go to the tree, pick up a pink Christmas ornament and hang it on a branch, which makes me feel worse. I walk down the hall and into my room. At least I'll have an hour to work.

My mother is still in her room. After she came home from the grocery store thirty minutes ago, I helped her carry six bags in from the car and then we put everything away. We barely spoke and now I'm feeling awful.

When we finished in the kitchen, I asked if she wanted to continue decorating the tree. She claimed she had a headache and was going to lie down. So I came back to the guest room and continued working, and I accomplished a lot. I get up from the desk, walk down the dimly lit hall to my mother's room. It's six-thirty. I tap gently on her bedroom door.

"Yes?"

"May I come in?"

"Certainly, Gwen."

I walk in, stop by the dresser to focus my eyes. Mother shifts a little on the bed, leans over and turns on her bedside lamp, the same one I used to turn on when I was living here. I'd sit where she is, on her bed, read and wait for her to come home.

"I fell asleep," she says.

Even so, she looks worn out. "You still look a little tired."

She touches her hair. "I probably do. I'm not as young as I used to be."

"Who is? I can't believe I'm forty."

She pats the edge of the bed and I sit next to her. Her room smells the same as it did when I lived here—clean, void of perfume—naked, cool air.

When I lived at home I used to come into her room in the early mornings, too, before I left for school. She sometimes worked evenings at the hospital. I'd tap on her door and cross the space between us, sit beside her. I liked being near her when she was home. I missed her so much. I guess I never got used to the loneliness of not having her around.

"I got a lot of the brief written while you were taking a nap," I say, hoping it will diminish the tension between us.

She reaches for my hand and rubs my fingers a little then lets go. "I hate to see you work so hard."

"Why is that? You, above anyone, should know about needing to work."

"Maybe that's why I hate to see it. I missed a lot of things in my life because of work."

I shift. "Well, people depend on me to represent them well. That takes work. I wouldn't want to let them down."

"But I know you. You go beyond what you have to do."

I move a little closer. "That's how I've gotten myself in the position to make partner so early."

"I do know something about ambition." She laughs gently.

The image, the one I used to think about when I was lying in this bed, pops into my head—my mother in the emergency room standing over a patient, the same worried look on her face that I see now. "You always were so determined," I say. "At night when you were gone, I'd imagine you saving lives, like on TV, yelling 'stat, get the cart!'"

She smiles again. "Well, it was never that dramatic, but at times there was a lot of pressure. Maybe too much."

"What do you mean by too much? I thought you were happy." I shift, touch her shoulder.

She folds her hands in her lap, smiles. "Work kept me from thinking about things, kept me from really living my life. Now I realize I was a workaholic. I should have demanded the hospital hire more staff."

Shock rolls across my chest. I always thought my mother worked hard only because she loved it. "I thought that was what your life was about. That you loved your work."

"I did love my work. But I didn't have to love it that much, work so many hours." She wets her bottom lip with the tip of her tongue. "I should have found a happy medium."

"Do you miss working now?" I ask.

"Yes, and now I have a lot of time to think about things since I'm not so distracted."

"What *things?*"

She shrugs her shoulders.

"Well, you could work part-time." And for the first time I realize it must be difficult for my mother—her entire life shifting with retirement.

"Maybe. I do want to keep my medical license current, but I noticed the last few years, my reflexes were getting a little slow. I'm not as quick as I used to be, so I certainly don't want to practice in the emergency room anymore, even part-time."

I take a deep breath, want to ask her again why she needed to be distracted, but we've never really talked a lot.

She sits up more. "Don't worry. I'm adjusting. I like the free time to relax, read." She gestures toward the stack of books on her nightstand. "I'll be fine. I want to do things I didn't have a chance to do before, like enjoying a holiday with my daughter." She pats my hand then looks toward the bedroom door. "What do you say we have a light dinner? I bought sliced ham and potato salad. Then we can finish decorating the tree. I read there's going to be some great Christmas music on the easy listening channel tonight. And *It's a Wonderful Life* comes on at nine o'clock on TBS. We could watch it together."

"I saw it when I was a kid," I say, feeling better.

"You know, I've never seen that movie."

"From what I can remember it's great. I love Jimmy Stewart." I get up and she stands and stretches.

"He plays the lead, right?"

"Mother, I can't believe you've never watched that movie." We walk out of the bedroom, down the hall and into the kitchen. I flip on the overhead light and we both blink.

"So you never saw *It's a Wonderful Life*, not even when you were a kid?"

"No. We didn't go to the movies because there was never any extra money. And we didn't have a TV. Besides, my father would not have approved."

"Really?" The only thing I remember about my grandfather was he was quiet. My mother, when he came to visit, would always talk about her work, tell him how well she was doing, and he'd just look at her, not say a word. And for the first time, I realize how odd that was. Most parents would act happy about their daughter's achievements.

She walks over to the refrigerator, pulls out bread, mayo, the ham slices. "Do you want mustard?" she asks.

"That's fine." I find plates, take them to the kitchen island, stand next to her as she places the iceberg lettuce next to the ham and mustard.

"Grandpa was so quiet. I never really knew him very well," I say, remembering he seldom visited.

"Yes, he was. Quiet, stern and I didn't know him well, either. But I do know he never forgave me for going to college, marrying your father or becoming a doctor."

"Really?" There is so much I don't know about my mother's life.

"He didn't want me to move away. He didn't have a

college education, and he didn't think his daughter needed one, either. But I knew it was my way out of poverty."

"I never knew that. How did you make it through school without his help?"

"I took out college loans and worked a full-time job." She places her hands on the counter, takes a deep breath.

"While you were going to college? Full time?" I lean against the counter, think about my college experience, how my mother insisted I not work, paid all the tuition.

"Yes. And the summers I had two jobs."

I expect her to have this grim expression, but instead she smiles at me. "Your grandfather did his best. He was left with five kids when my mother died. A milkman didn't make much money in those days. And five kids probably ate him out of house and home."

I nod, feel a little ashamed that I didn't know how tough my mother had it. I always thought her childhood was better than mine because she had a father and I didn't. Plus she had brothers and sisters and I imagined everyone happy, together, never lonely.

"What about your brothers and sisters?" I ask.

"Oh, we got along, but I was the youngest and they all had to work. We were so poor." My mother begins dishing out the potato salad. I look at her hands and realize they are more wrinkled, and her fingers don't look as long as I remembered them, but they are the same hands that were saving lives a few months ago.

CHAPTER 4

Bing Crosby is singing "White Christmas" and my mother is wrestling with our Christmas tree. After dinner she suggested we finish decorating the tree. I figured with the two of us, we could put on the ornaments in no time, throw a bunch of tinsel on the branches and then I could head back to my room and continue working.

But it didn't happen that way.

First we rearranged the chilli lights to fit the tree but every time I hung an ornament, my mother would frown and say how awful the tree looked. I tried to encourage her, but she just frowned more, so it took longer than I expected.

And then the chilli peppers died.

"What do you think is wrong with them?" I ask.

"I have no idea," she says.

I bend down, unplug the strand of lights and then plug them in again, hold my breath, and hope they light up. They don't.

"Well, they aren't working, that's for sure. What should we do now?" I ask as I stand and face her.

She stops shaking a strand of lights, studies the tree then

crosses her arms. "I guess we'll have to take the lights off, then try to find more."

"That's not going to be easy." I go to the tree and pull an ornament off. It's covered in tinsel. I pull the tinsel off and place the ornament in the flimsy carton on the floor.

"We could try the drugstore on the corner. They might have some Christmas things," she says, stepping back and continuing to stare at the tree.

I look at the clock on the bookshelf. "Mother, it's nine o'clock, December twenty-third. Do you think they'll have anything left or even be open?"

"They're open twenty-four hours a day. I can call and see if they have lights."

"I was planning on reviewing some cases tonight, but…" More tension attacks my neck and shoulders.

"You could work tomorrow."

I take a deep breath. "No, I can't. You want us to go shopping."

"I know your work is important, but it's so close to Christmas. I'd like to have the tree decorated in time. Tomorrow we could leave a little later so you can work in the morning. I really wanted the tree to be perfect for Christmas Eve." Her hopeful tone pulls at my heart.

"A few years ago you would have been happy I was working a little more. Hell, a few years ago you wouldn't have even been here." A small bit of anger thumps inside my chest and I cross my arms in an effort to bury it.

She stares at me, presses her lips together. "I know my priorities were different before I retired."

"My clients need me. You know it's really bugging me that all of a sudden you want me to stop what I'm doing just because it's Christmas. You never did."

"I just don't want you to one day turn around and…"

"And what?" I ask, somewhat breathless.

"You just need to find a happy medium with work and fun. I don't want you to make the same mistakes I did."

I go to the couch. "I'm close to making partner. I don't want to blow that." I sit on the couch, cross my arms again and stare at the tree.

"Well, okay. I'll run over to the drugstore now and then decorate the tree. You go *work*," she says, but I can see from her expression she's not happy. I get up.

"I don't want you to go to the drugstore alone this late. I'll go with you." I smile to hide my frustration.

She shakes her head. "No, you work. I really don't want you to go." And before I can say another word she walks into the kitchen. I take a deep breath, try to calm my pounding heart, follow her, but she's already in the garage. I hear the garage door open.

"Great," I say, opening the door, walking into the garage. My mother sees me, stops the car and rolls down her window. The balmy night air finds me, and I go over to her.

"I'm going with you," I say.

"Fine."

* * *

We came back from the drugstore fifteen minutes ago with a trunkful of Christmas decorations. I carried the lights and ornaments in the house and placed them by the tree while my mother made hot chocolate and turned on Christmas music. Mom walks into the living room, hands me a steaming mug of hot chocolate. We only spoke a little while we were picking out decorations, and there's still this thick tension between us.

"Isn't it wonderful we found white Christmas lights and so many of them?" she says.

"We should have gone there in the first place." I take a sip of my chocolate. It's very good—nice and sweet, creamy, just hot enough, and it melts a little of my frustration.

"Look at it this way. If we would have gone there first we wouldn't appreciate these as much." She gestures to the stacked boxes of white ornaments, then takes a sip of her hot chocolate.

"But I would be working tonight and wouldn't be worrying." I laugh, hope she does, too, but she doesn't even smile.

"You go work, I'll decorate."

"No, I'll help," I say. I'm not used to my mother looking so sad. "I'll just work a little later tonight."

"Are you sure?"

I nod. "This hot chocolate's really good." I raise my mug.

"Thanks. Yesterday, right before I called you to come home for the holiday, I imagined you and I drinking hot chocolate, decorating the tree, listening to music. Just like this. Isn't it wonderful we can do it?"

"It is." I make myself sound happy, fight the frustration still in my chest, try not to think about how I should be working.

"Can you believe the drugstore even had white Christmas ornaments? Who would have thought that a drugstore would have so many Christmas decorations?" She opens one of the boxes of white lights.

"We got lucky."

When we got to the drugstore, not only did we find white lights, we found white ornaments, too. My mother was going to pay for all the decorations, but she had already spent three hundred dollars at Wal-Mart, so I insisted that I buy them, probably out of guilt for being so cranky with her.

Since everything was half-off, we loaded up a cart with seven sets of white lights and seven boxes of ornaments and I paid one hundred and fifty-nine dollars at the register. A bargain compared to the red chillies.

"We should take everything off the tree, then we can start fresh," she says.

"Okay." I grab a pink Christmas ornament, unhook it from the branch, and my mother begins pulling tinsel off the tree.

"I think if we're careful, we can reuse the tinsel." She shakes a handful at me.

"We have plenty of new tinsel. It'll be faster if we just add some."

She touches my arm, really looks at me. "The white lights and the white ornaments are going to look so good. Do you think you'll like the tree?"

To my surprise I feel a little excited. "Yes, I've always wanted a big, real tree, decorated just this way." "White Christmas" begins to play from the radio.

"I'm dreaming of a white Christmas," my mother sings. She has a very nice voice. I take another ornament and place it in the box and smile at her. She stops singing, stares at me for a moment. "What?"

"I never realized what a good singing voice you have. Isn't that odd? We've known each other for forty years and I can't remember you ever singing in this house."

"Thank you. I guess I didn't sing much, did I…?" She trails off, then starts to sing again. "May your days be merry and bright."

"And may all your Christmases be white," I sing badly, pull another ornament off the tree, feel more relaxed than I've felt since I got here.

"Well, that's one thing you didn't inherit from me," she says.

I laugh. "But I inherited a lot of other things. We certainly look alike."

"We used to. I'm a little older now."

"Mother, you look great."

"So do you. I can't understand why you don't have a boyfriend."

Her comment startles me a little. She's never seemed to

worry about my social life before. "It's by choice, believe me." I pull another ornament off the tree, look at her again. "By the way, you don't have one, either," I say in defense.

A memory sneaks in. My mother sitting on the couch late at night, looking so lonely. And suddenly I want to know why she never dated, never married after my father died. "Can I ask you something?"

The tree is almost bare of ornaments.

"Of course. I thought you knew you can ask me anything." She rests her hands on her hips, studies the tree.

"I never felt like I could," I say and for the first time in my life I feel like I'm opening up to her.

"Could what?"

"Could ask you anything. We never really ever talked that much."

Her eyes grow wide then she walks over to the couch and sits. "I thought we had good communication."

I open up the box of white lights and unwind the strand. We didn't. We never had time, but I don't want to say this because I'm afraid it will hurt her feelings. "I'll start with the top again, but first I'm going to plug them all in, make sure they work." I move to the light socket, plug the lights in, and they pop on, glimmer. To my surprise I feel another thump of childish excitement. "Oh, aren't they pretty? I love white Christmas lights."

"Gwen?"

I look over at her. "Yes?"

"You said you wanted to ask me something. I know you believe we didn't talk a lot when you were younger. Well—maybe we could start now. You know that old adage, 'It's never too late.' I mean, the tree is a good example of that. We didn't think we'd get it the way we wanted it, and—" she gestures to the lights "—it looks like it's going to be wonderful."

"We aren't there yet." I shake my head, laugh.

"But don't you think it's going to be a pretty tree?"

"Don't count your chickens—"

"I'm amazed." She shakes her head. "I never realized, but you're very negative. Why is that?"

I can't deny that I am. Have I always been negative? I unplug the lights, move to the tree and begin winding them around the top. When I was a kid I remember having a lot of hope.

"Do you think you're negative?" she asks again.

I turn to her. "I think I'm realistic. I'm a lawyer. You know how realistic you have to be to practice law? It's a survival technique."

"Realistic and negative are two very different outlooks. There were a lot of bad scenes in the hospital, but I was never negative."

"Mother, I don't know how you were. We never had time to get to know each other. For example, I thought you'd be happy that I'm working hard." I step back, fight the now-familiar anger growing in my stomach.

"Well, I am, but..." She crosses her arms. "It's just...well, it's Christmas. People need to relax, take some time off." She stands, comes over to the tree and begins pulling at the new lights. Then she plugs them in.

"They work!" She looks at me.

"In a matter of days you've turned into Kris Kringle." I gesture to the tree, the lights and ornaments.

"I realize I made mistakes. Plus, I have the time now for Christmas. I didn't when I was practicing. I should have taken time...and I just don't want you to make the same mistakes I did."

I shake my head. "That's the past. There's nothing we can do about it. And I don't look at me working hard as a mistake. Plus I don't have a child or anyone I'm really close to in Boston."

"I...well..." Her expression turns to hurt. "But you have me. Sometimes a change of heart is good, don't you think? I thought you'd be happy that I had one."

I force a grin. "I've just got to get used to it, that's all. You went from not giving a damn to really caring about the holiday and that's a hard leap. Plus I don't understand the change."

She moves to the couch, sits. "A few days ago I was thinking about how I was always so busy. Then I remembered when I was little we didn't celebrate Christmas. My father took the extra milk routes on Christmas Eve day and Christmas. He didn't have time for any decorating or presents. I guess he was too busy trying to make ends meet. I grew up believing that work was the most important thing in life. I guess like my father believed."

I take a few steps toward her then stop, swallow, feel a little embarrassed that I felt angry. "I didn't know any of that."

She looks at me, surprise filling her gaze. "I never talked about that part of my life because I wanted to forget it. When I was little, on Christmas morning we'd wait for my father to come home and sometimes the one treat we got was hot chocolate. He'd bring an extra bottle of chocolate milk home and heat it up for us." She glances at our mugs on the coffee table. "It was such a nice treat. And then we'd sing, and my father would tell me I had the nicest voice of all. That's about the only time he ever complimented me."

"Really?" My heart aches more, and I remember how my mother was always so good with praise.

She nods. "My father was like that. He didn't have any spirit. Maybe he was tired or lost hope. When I got older and your father and I got married, he tried to make up for what I didn't have as a child. One time I admired a watch. It was in one of those pretty little shops by the college. The face was surrounded by rhinestones. And he bought it for me!" She grins. "I knew he couldn't afford it. He was barely making ends meet. I took it back and gave him the money and said all I wanted was a cup of hot chocolate. And that night, I think it was Christmas Eve, we went to this little restaurant and drank hot chocolate."

"Oh, Mother," I say, fighting the lump growing in my throat.

"Oh, your father and I were happy. We just didn't have a lot of money. I guess that's why I worked so hard, so I could give you more of what I didn't have. At one time I thought hard work was the most important thing in a person's life. And I tried to teach you that, too, since your father wasn't here."

I think about my father—a man I never knew—how every year I wished he could be with us.

To fight the sad memory, I get up, string another set of lights on the tree, and then unwind the third set, check them, then begin wrapping the strand around the branches.

"You know," I say, "I always thought about Dad around Christmas. And when I did, well, I always felt lonely. You rarely mentioned him and when you did, you looked so sad."

She stares at me, blinks as if she's trying to remember something. "When we were young, in college and poor, your father and I always talked about how our Christmases would be when we had our own family. We'd laugh and even plan what presents we'd buy…he always had these great dreams about what he was going to buy me when we had money." She stops, looks at the tree. "You know, I haven't thought about that watch in a very long time."

"I wish we would have talked about these things before," I say.

"I know, but one thing, Gwen," my mother says as I reach for another box of lights. "I'll Be Home For Christmas" begins playing from the radio. A huge lump forms in my throat. My mother sings along for a few moments.

"What were you going to say?" I manage.

"When I was raising you, it wasn't easy for me to admit I

was wrong, because I learned in medical school, if I was wrong it might kill someone."

"I know. You told me that years ago."

"Well…I was wrong. Hard work is not the most *important* aspect of life."

I plug another set of lights in and they snap on. "And what is the most important thing in life, Mother?" I look over to where she's sitting. For the first time I realize how she must have struggled through life. I used to think she was so in control, her life moving so smoothly. But now I see she was hiding a lot of sadness.

"Being with your family is important, more so than work. I missed so much of your growing up."

"But when there are deadlines or people dying," I say, gesturing back to my room, "so many people counting on you, it's hard to believe that. You have the luxury of time now, retirement. I don't."

"I was just hoping it wouldn't be too late. Someday you'll understand." She stands, picks up our hot chocolate mugs and walks into the kitchen.

A moment later I hear her bedroom door close.

I walk over to the radio and click it off, then walk back to the couch and sit. Why is my mother telling me all these things now? Six month ago she didn't even seem to care. I stand to fight my aggravation, go to the tree and hang an ornament on it. I should go to work but I know I won't be able to concentrate.

Forty-five minutes later the tree is decorated. I step back, turn off the lights by the couch and the room fills with delicate white light. I go into the kitchen, find the white wine in the refrigerator and pour myself a glass. I take a sip and it feels cold against my tongue. In the living room the tree looks like the one I imagined as a child—magical, glowing. I sit on the couch and take another sip of wine. The tree certainly turned out better than I thought it would. I'd love to share it with my mother, but I know she's tired and I don't want to bother her.

CHAPTER 5

December 24

"Are you ready?" my mother asks, then checks the kitchen clock. "It's almost eleven." We are both standing in the kitchen dressed in T-shirts, jeans and tennis shoes.

She seems more rested than she did last night and I'm thankful for that. However there is still this little undercurrent of tension between us—as if we're angry but not talking about it. And I'm not used to this. When I lived at home, before I graduated from college, my mother was so involved in her work there was never time for fights or disagreements.

"I'll just finish my coffee," I say, working to sound upbeat. I don't want to go Christmas shopping, but I know if I say so it will hurt her feelings, and I certainly don't want to do that again.

I place my coffee mug on the kitchen counter, try to feel excited about our shopping trip, but I'm not looking forward to the crowds and the constant Christmas music.

Mom smiles at me then walks out of the kitchen. Last

night after I decorated the tree, I went to my room and worked till two this morning. I got a lot done but even though I slept in, I'm tired.

"Gwen, come here."

"What's wrong?" I ask as I walk into the living room.

She's standing in the middle of the room, gazing at the tree. The lights are on and even with the late-morning sun blazing through the window, the tree looks great.

I stand next to her.

"You did a wonderful job with the tree," she says then turns and hugs me. "I'm sorry I didn't help last night but I was tired."

I know this isn't true—she was mad at me. "Do you feel rested?" I ask anyway.

"I do. I have my list ready. I'm so excited about shopping. Music will be playing in the stores, and it'll be so festive!" She gestures to the tree. "And the tree is ready for presents."

"You know the stores are going to be crowded?"

"But isn't that the fun of Christmas? All the people, everyone happy, the music?"

"I'm not sure I'd call it *the fun*."

She forces a smile. "Well, at least the tree is done the way we want it. We both need to buy Janie a present. I went shopping for you before you got here."

"You did?"

"Yes, the morning we talked and you said you couldn't come visit. I thought if I went shopping then maybe you might change your mind. It was kind of like making a wish."

I stare at her, raise an eyebrow. "You've never been superstitious before, or at least I never thought you were. You were always the scientist."

She presses her lips together, frowns a little. "I wouldn't call it superstitious. I was hopeful. I used to be that way when I was a kid. I guess I lost it as I grew up. Too much work takes a lot away from a person."

I turn a little, close my eyes for a moment. I will not get upset! I will not even if she mentions work a hundred times.

"Gwen. What's wrong?"

"Nothing, you just keep harping on the work thing."

"I'm only trying to help you." She walks over and touches a tree branch. "You know, we forgot to get something to go around the bottom of the tree when we were at the Wal-Mart yesterday." She points to the green metal tree stand.

"Do we really need something?" Another small wave of frustration begins to rise in my stomach. I don't want to spend all day Christmas shopping. "We could use a white sheet. I've seen people drape them around the bottoms of trees."

She shakes her head. "It wouldn't look as nice."

"Who cares? It's just the two of us and Janie, on Christmas Day, and you know she won't care. I don't care."

More disappointment grows in her expression and this makes me feel awful. I shake my head. "Okay, so we'll pick up a thing to go around the tree while we're out."

She smiles. "Good, and by tonight everything will be perfect." She smiles.

"Nothing is ever perfect, Mom. Perfection is an illusion!" My words come out harsher than I want them to but I can't stop myself. "It either works or it doesn't. What in the hell is ever perfect?"

"Well…" Her eyes grow wide. "Maybe we shouldn't go shopping. You seem so angry."

"I'm not angry, I'm frustrated. And if I stay home I'll feel guilty about not going shopping. We're going shopping and we're going to have a good time doing it, too."

We are standing in the handbag section of Dillard's department store. The store is mobbed with shoppers buying last-minute Christmas gifts. Right now my mother is at the cash register paying for her part of Janie's gift. We've been here three hours, and just a few minutes ago we found the *right* Coach handbag with matching wallet and key chain to give to Janie tomorrow. We had to go to three different stores because everything is so picked over.

My mother walks over to me with a large shopping bag in her left hand and a huge smile on her face. "Well, it's good we got that done. Now we need to split up." She re-situates the bag.

"Let me help with that." Before she can object I take the bag from her. "I thought we were finished," I say over the loud Christmas music.

"Of course we aren't finished. I didn't see any packages in your suitcase."

I raise an eyebrow. "I know. I was so busy before I left I

didn't have time to shop. I'm surprised you bought me something. We haven't exchanged presents in years." And suddenly there is a lump in my throat. Maybe it's because I just realized my favorite Christmas song, "Silver Bells," is playing or maybe it's because I'm thinking about the last three Christmases I spent alone in Boston after I broke up with Aaron. Last year, on Christmas Day, after I worked from five till noon, I sat in my living room watching it snow and telling myself I was silly to even care about Christmas. But deep down I felt lonely and sad.

"I really love this song," I say, trying to distract myself from the way I feel.

My mother turns her head a little then smiles. "Oh, 'Silver Bells.' It is lovely, isn't it?"

I nod. The first time I heard "Silver Bells" I was in seventh grade. The choir put on a Christmas pageant, and a friend of mine, Claire Simmons, sang the song so sweetly. When she finished, I clapped until my hands hurt. She was such a good friend and I was so proud of her. After the show I went home with her family, and their house looked like a winter wonderland. Claire and I sat by the tree, and she sang the song again, then her mother brought us cookies and eggnog. Ever since I graduated from law school I haven't had time for friends, a social life—any life at all except work. I guess I miss that more than I realized.

"Silver bells, silver bells, it's Christmas time in the city," my mother sings perfectly.

"Ring-a-ling, ring-a-ling," I sing off-key then laugh at how bad I sound.

A woman pushes me a little to get past. "Excuse me!" I look at her. She is carrying too many shopping bags, her face is red and she looks so frustrated I feel sorry for her.

"I'm sorry," I say. I take my mother's arm, guide her away from the crowded aisle to the wall of handbags we just spent thirty minutes going through. I gesture toward the store. "It's so crowded, are you sure you want to shop more? I certainly don't."

"You're right, I don't need anything for Christmas," she says, but I see more disappointment in her eyes.

I take a deep breath, try to push back the now familiar frustration that's in my chest. Why all these changes now? Why couldn't we have celebrated Christmas when I was younger and wanted to?

"But I have to do a little more shopping, for the secretaries at the hospital," she says. "Why don't we meet back here in thirty minutes? You can relax on a bench in the mall."

"Can you find everything in that amount of time?" I ask.

"Yes. I just need a few things. You can enjoy the decorations and stay out of the crowds."

"Okay." I smile despite the way I feel, knowing I'll spend my time searching for a gift.

My mother and I are standing in the living room.

"I thought tonight we'd go to the Christmas caroling party downtown," my mother says. "It starts at five and then we can come back here, have a quick dinner, then go to church." She shows me the newspaper ad for the caroling party that the city is sponsoring. The tree is plugged in and it looks even prettier than it did this morning.

"Mom, I haven't been to church in thirty years. We've shopped, decorated and listened to more Christmas music than should be legal. You know they've figured out that Christmas music causes depression." I stop myself from adding that I'm beginning to feel depressed, too.

"Who are *they?*"

"I don't know. Someone who did a study."

She shakes the ad at me. "Anybody can do a study and make the results come out the way they want them to. But this might be fun." She points to the paper again. "Caroling will get us more in the mood."

"I promise, I'm in the mood. Is it so important we spend two hours singing songs I don't even like? Plus I haven't wrapped your present yet." I gesture to the small pile of shopping bags lying on the kitchen table. While my mother was shopping, I managed to buy her a large black purse and matching wallet that I'm not sure she's even going to like. But I found it at a cash register that didn't have much of a line.

She stares at me. "This morning you said you weren't going to shop any more."

"I changed my mind."

"I see. And in Dillard's you said you liked 'Silver Bells.'

You even sang a few bars. And what's Christmas without carols and a church service?" She shakes the paper at me.

Suddenly I'm thinking about Claire, how well she sang and how hopeful I felt that evening. Where did all that hope go?

"Christmas carols really make the holiday. What would it be without them?" she asks.

"Calm, peaceful. They depress me," I say too fast. I don't want to think about all the unhappy Christmases I've spent.

"They do?"

"Yes, they do." I cross my arms. "I don't have a lot of happy memories of Christmas."

"I know. That's why I wanted to celebrate this year. We can make new memories."

"I need to make *new* legal briefs." I cross the living room, sit on the couch.

"Gwen, it's almost Christmas Eve. Most people at least take today and tomorrow off."

"You never did, and I'm not most people."

"Can't you try to relax, dear, just for tonight and enjoy the holiday?"

I look at her, try to hide my disbelief. "That's not what you did when you were my age." The statement comes out too imposing and I didn't mean it to be. But I don't want to go caroling and think about Christmas pasts. "I'm sorry, but all of a sudden it's like you're on this mission to have this *perfect Christmas*, which by the way, I don't believe can ever happen."

She glances at the tree. "Life is how you look at it. I'm finding that out very quickly. Especially since I retired. Perfect is a state of mind."

"Maybe." I work to hold back the anger that keeps churning in my chest, but for some reason I can't seem to bury it.

"You know, with my work there was never enough time to enjoy life. But I've realized I was hiding behind my work and I think you're doing the same thing."

I shake my head. "What? No, I'm not! I like working."

"I did, too, but I also used my work so I didn't have to think about the holidays. And that's what you're doing now." She takes a deep breath. "And I don't want you to miss this part of life because I was so stupid and couldn't face the sadness." And then she sighs.

"What sadness? And why are you sighing all the time?"

"I didn't know I was. Maybe because I feel sad. But there's nothing I can do about the past. I'm only trying to make this year better." She turns, comes to the couch and sits.

"The tree turned out nice," I say, trying to make up for my crankiness and maybe make her feel better.

She nods. "I'm sorry. I'm a little emotional right now."

"Why is that? I hope you know I appreciate everything you've done. It's just all this Christmas stuff is weird."

"I do. But a few weeks ago I realized I didn't have to work so much. And I regret that. It's just I...don't want you to be my age and look back with regret."

I fully face her, feel better that at least we're talking. "I'm not sure regretting things from the past is very productive or even my style, Mom."

"I didn't think it was mine, either. I thought I wanted success, and I knew my job was important. I was so poor as a kid, and I didn't want that for you. I just focused on the wrong things. And last night after I went to bed early, I realized I hid behind my work so I didn't have to face my sad feelings." She reaches over and squeezes my hand. "I should have realized some of the things I missed and then made sure you didn't miss them, too. But I just couldn't see that far. I guess it was because of the way I was raised. I mean, a lot of things come from our childhoods, don't they?" she asks.

I nod as a nice warmth fills my chest. "They say they do. But I don't know who *they* are." We both laugh and it feels good. "I had no idea what your life was like when you were a child, Mom. I mean, we've never really talked about it until yesterday."

"Probably because I was too damn busy. Or maybe I just didn't want to think or talk about my past."

"But, Mother, you helped a lot of people by being at the hospital, by working so hard."

She nods, rubs her forehead then smiles. "I did help a lot of people, didn't I, but at your expense?"

"Oh, I did okay. I'm happy, successful. I never had any college debt. You made sure of that. I went to a great school. Some of my friends are still paying off their student loans."

"You were such a serious child, but very good. I never had to worry about you."

I smile, gesture to the kitchen. "Speaking of worry, do you think the turkey will unfreeze by tomorrow? It feels like it's still frozen."

"I have no idea. I don't know a lot about turkeys."

"Neither do I, but I guess we can always order a pizza."

We both laugh again. "Not much of a Christmas dinner with a pizza," she says.

I look at the tree, and for the first time in days I feel happy. "But the people you're with are what's important about Christmas—not the trappings, the gifts, the food."

"You're right." She looks around the living room.

"You seem lonely, Mom."

"Well, sometimes…retirement, it's a different lifestyle. There's a lot of time to think, to remember—maybe too much." She leans back, closes her eyes.

"Yesterday, you never explained why you never dated. Is it something you don't want to talk about?"

She opens her eyes, rubs her forehead again with her fingertips and looks at me. "I loved your father so much. We knew each other since high school. I think I was the poorest girl in the school, but he loved me, anyway, despite how I dressed and looked."

"Was he poor, too?"

"No, he came from a middle-class family. His father was an engineer, which was a pretty good job in those days."

"I remember you telling me that." I don't have any of my own memories of my father—just the faded photograph my mother still has on her dresser—my father looking so serious, sitting at a desk, a pencil behind his ear. When I lived at home my mother kept a photo on my nightstand—him holding me when I was about two weeks old. Now it sits on my dresser in Boston. "You were high school sweethearts, right?" I ask and an image of my parents, hopeful, in love, comes into my mind.

"We were. Well, as much as we could be in those days. My father wouldn't let me date, but then when we went to college, your father and I became very close. I wanted to get married, so Alex agreed and we eloped. I worked in a pharmaceutical lab and he started med school."

I stand to fight the lump in my throat, realize how much I miss having a father. I cross the room, find the stereo and turn it on. "Silver Bells" begins to play. And for the first time in a long time, I wonder what our lives would have been like if my father were alive. I shake the thought away because it hurts too much to think about. I turn back to the radio, turn it off and glance at my mother who is still sitting on the couch.

She gestures toward the radio. "'Silver Bells' was your father's favorite song, too. When you said that at the department store this afternoon it brought back so many memories. I almost told you I wanted to come home. After your father passed away the only way I could survive my grief was to work as hard as I possibly could. I guess I got in that habit and never got out of it, especially around the holidays."

I rub my face, think about my mother—a young woman, all alone, her heart broken, trying to raise a child, hiding behind her work.

She smiles. "I should have told you that yesterday, about 'Silver Bells' and how your father loved it, but I didn't want to spoil our mood, our fun. I have so many memories of him."

I go back to the couch, sit next to her. "Share something else with me."

"Well, when we were going to college we'd take walks on chilly nights in the fall, and he would ask me to sing. He always requested 'Silver Bells' and he'd always say how he loved my voice.

"You know I realized last night after I went to bed, I stopped singing after he died. Maybe I just didn't feel like singing anymore."

She reaches over and pats my fingers. Her skin feels so warm.

"You never thought about marrying again?" I ask.

"I worked too much and I knew I'd never find a man like your father. At times, you remind me so much of him. He was serious, yet fun. Plus, my father, after my mother passed away, would bring women home, and I felt ignored when he did that. I would get mad and wonder how he could betray my mother. I never wanted you to feel that way."

I nod, realize how she tried to do the right things for me, even though she wasn't home much. "I didn't really know Dad, so maybe I wouldn't have felt that way if you would have had a date," I say.

She turns her head a little. "I guess I should have reminded myself that you didn't have the same feelings for him that I did. You were only a year old. Then I started med school. I wanted to finish for your father's sake. He wanted so much to be a doctor."

"Was it your dream, too?" I ask, wanting to know more.

"After he died it was. He used to talk about working in an emergency room, helping people. We were so serious when we were young. I was going to work until he got out of med school, then I was going to stay home, have more babies and keep house."

I smile. "I can't imagine you doing that."

"Your father and I wanted three children. He was so dedicated to family and medicine. After, something in me changed and I just wanted to keep his dream alive."

"What did he think about me?" I ask, try to imagine a man I never knew.

"Oh, he was crazy about you. He used to pick you up out of the crib, hold you over his head and you'd laugh, then he'd laugh."

For a few moments we sit quietly.

"It must have been hard to be alone so young and for so long with a child," I finally say.

She studies me, her eyes wide. "It was at first. I was so naive, but I had you to care for. You're alone now, too. Isn't it difficult for you?"

I laugh, think of all the boyfriends I've had. How three

years ago after the hurtful breakup with Aaron, I swore I'd never date again. "Oh, Mother, I've had a ton of boyfriends. My last breakup was tough. Right now I don't want to date for a long time. Plus, I work so much. Maybe someday, you know?"

"Don't wall yourself off like I did. The more you do, the easier it is to do. When I was your age, I didn't know how fast life goes by. One day you'll turn around and twenty years will have passed and it'll seem like the blink of an eye."

I sit up straighter, clasp my hands together. "You know you could start dating. You have the time now."

"At my age?" Her hand goes to her chest. "Wouldn't that bother you?"

"No, I wouldn't mind at all. And sixty-five is considered young these days. It's the new fifty."

"I don't think you can teach an old dog new tricks."

"That's the present I'll ask for next Christmas. You going out on a date and telling me about it. Woof, woof," I say then laugh.

"Next Christmas…that's a long ways off. That's why I wanted this one to be perfect." She gets off the couch, looks down at me. "Maybe you should go work on your brief. I know it's worrying you."

I stand and hug her, feel warm and calm inside and want to do something nice for her. "I have to go to Kinko's. Can I borrow your car?"

"Of course," she says, "But—"

"Great. I'll be back before you know it."

* * *

I'm in Dillard's department store exchanging my mother's Christmas present. The store is packed with last-minute shoppers and the Christmas music is on full blast. On the drive over I racked my brain trying to think of something I could buy my mother—something she would like—and then as I pulled into the parking lot it hit me.

I walk through the crowded aisles, smile at people who I make eye contact with. I go to the counter where I'm hoping to find her gift, and suddenly my heart feels as if it's going to burst with happiness. "Silver Bells" is playing over the loudspeaker, and for the first time in years I'm enjoying Christmas.

CHAPTER 6

Christmas Day

I'm still in bed. Last night after I got home from Dillard's, I wrapped my mother's new gift. And I was in such a good mood when I finished, I suggested we go Christmas caroling. Her eyes grew bigger, like a kid's, and she said she couldn't believe I wanted to go. Then she asked me if I was sure. I nodded and laughed. And to my surprise we had a wonderful time. When we got to the town center, there were about fifty people standing around, laughing, talking and having a good time. Parents had brought their children, and there were a few older adults with grandchildren.

Right on time the person in charge handed out small songbooks, lit some candles and we all began singing. I listened to my mother's voice—so crystal clear, pretty, and I thought of my father, how he liked her voice. Plus the Christmas music didn't bother me. In fact I found it soothing, and suddenly I felt lit up inside. And a gentle hope filled my chest and mixed with crisp excitement. Then we began singing

"Jingle Bells" and I stepped closer to my mother, put my arm around her and sang as loud as I could.

I hear my mother in the kitchen. I climb out of bed, pad down the hall and find her.

"Merry Christmas," I say, yawning.

She's standing at the sink looking at the turkey. She turns. "Merry Christmas." But she doesn't look happy.

"What's wrong?" And I realize how odd it feels to ask my mother this question. She's always been the one who's fine, the one who never had a problem.

"The turkey…it's still frozen." She knocks on it with a clenched fist. "You were right to worry."

"It didn't defrost yet? My God, how long should it take?" I cross the kitchen to the sink.

"The directions said three days in the fridge. What do we do now?"

I look around. The warm Florida sun is illuminating the kitchen as if it's summer. I don't have any idea how to fix a frozen turkey.

"If it were just the two of us…but Janie is coming over and I was hoping…" she says, shifting her gaze to the sink.

"I'll run to the store and buy another turkey."

"The ones in the grocery store are all frozen." She crosses her arms, looks desolate, and this makes me feel awful. We were so happy last night and I felt so hopeful.

"Mother, it's only a turkey. We have everything else. Janie will understand." I go to the fridge, look in and find a package of turkey slices. "Look, we have turkey. We can make the rest of the meal and still have turkey…sandwiches!"

My mother shakes her head. I go to the coffee pot, fill my mug and take a sip. "Well, the coffee's great."

"Thanks. But this is not how I was planning Christmas Day. I wanted the house to smell like turkey, and then we were going to make the other things together, sit at the table and laugh."

"We can still do some of it, like laugh. It's just a turkey, not the end of the world. We shouldn't care."

"But it's Christmas Day and we always made turkey on Christmas Day."

"We?" I raise an eyebrow, laugh.

"Well, we always *had* turkey." She crosses her arms.

"I don't know why we can't put the turkey in the oven and let it cook. I mean it will take longer, but I'm sure it will be fine." I look at the kitchen clock. "We've got plenty of time."

"Do you think that would work?" She glances past me to the oven.

"I can call Janie and ask her."

"This early?" she asks.

"You know she's up. She's always up early." I go to the phone, pick it up and a few minutes later I'm helping my mother load the turkey in the oven.

"Janie said it wouldn't kill us so that's good," I say.

"I wouldn't want to poison anyone on Christmas Day, for God's sake." My mother laughs.

"You won't. We had such a nice time last night. Let's open our gifts, then we'll cook, and when Janie gets here, it'll be fun."

"That's fine." She crosses the space to the coffee pot, pours herself another cup. We go into the living room. She's turned on the tree and the room looks pretty. And to my surprise, I feel almost the same excitement I felt when I was a kid on Christmas morning.

"Okay, I'm ready to open presents!" I rub my hands together as more excitement streams through my body. I kneel, get her gift from under the tree and bring it to her, then we both sit on the couch.

"I thought you said I didn't need anything?" She looks at the small box I wrapped last night, shakes it a little and smiles.

"I changed my mind. Wait a minute." I get up, turn on the Christmas music, come back to the couch and sit next to her. "Okay, now you can open it."

"I thought you were tired of Christmas music?"

"After last night I have a new appreciation." "O Holy Night" is playing, and to my surprise it makes me feel more relaxed.

She pulls the paper away from her present then takes the lid off the black leather box. "Oh my, Gwen, you shouldn't have."

"I wanted to," I say, lean over and hug her. "I think my dad would want you to have it." My heart beats hard with emotion.

My mother takes the diamond wristwatch out of the box, wraps it gently around her left wrist then stares at it. "It's beautiful. I don't think I've ever had a nicer present."

I take a deep breath to fight the lump growing in my throat. "Maybe the one Dad gave you was nicer, but those are real diamonds. It's time you had a nice watch. No pun intended." Yesterday I realized with my father gone, there was never anyone to give my mother anything special.

"It's really lovely."

"I'm glad you like it."

"Oh, I do. But it's too much," she says, shaking her head.

"Not at all. I think I owe you a few presents. I make good money."

"You don't owe me anything." She closes the clasp on the watch, then holds her arm out and stares at it. "It fits perfectly."

"Maybe you can wear it on your *date?*" I say, chuckling.

She turns a little. "What date?"

I laugh again, feel wonderful. "Last night I thought, well, you should think about being more social now that you're retired. I don't want to interfere, but you could go on a date. That's what I'm going to ask for as one of my Christmas gifts next year."

"Me going on a date for a present?"

I nod. "Yes, you going on a date."

"I think you should be the one to date," she says, leaning over and patting my shoulder.

"I'll have to think about that. Maybe next year." But my heart begins to pound with fear.

"Next year? That seems like a long ways off, doesn't it?" She turns a little, stares at her watch.

"Not really. Next Christmas is just around the corner. Honestly, you need a social life."

"I'll have to think about it." She touches her watch with the tip of her index finger. "How about opening your presents?"

"Presents?"

"One present is just something I found. It's yours, but I wrapped it." She stands, goes to the tree, picks up two packages, one large, one small. Then she stops and looks at her watch again. "This is so beautiful, Gwen. It's really too much, though."

"No, it isn't. And I'm glad you like it."

She comes back to the couch and hands me the larger package. I smile at her, feel so happy she likes her gift. "Should I open mine now?" I shake the package.

"Of course."

I carefully pull the red paper away, then take the lid off the large box. It's an outfit—a beautiful aquamarine silk blouse and cream-colored slacks—something I would never buy for myself but I love. "They're beautiful. I never have time for shopping. These are wonderful."

"Not as nice as my watch, but I saw the outfit on a mannequin weeks ago, and it reminded me of you. Maybe you can wear it out."

I smile. "Like I go out so much."

"Gwen, remember what I said." She stares out the window to the front yard. "I regret not spending more time with you."

"Oh, I was well taken care of, happy. We can make up for it now. Maybe next Christmas you can come to Boston. It will probably snow and that would be fun."

She sighs, doesn't look at me. "Next year, that seems like such a long time from today." Then she turns to me. "But you're here now, and we should be happy about that. Except for the turkey, everything turned out perfect."

And suddenly she looks so sad.

"Mother." I put my arm around her shoulders and hug her, realize I don't do this enough. "The turkey will be fine."

She sighs again, then sniffs.

"You aren't crying, are you?" And I feel helpless.

"No. I'm fine."

I lean back. "You look so sad."

"I'm fine. Here. Open your other present." She hands me the smaller gift.

"Okay," I say, and begin pulling the wrapping paper off.

"I found it when I was going through some boxes in the garage."

And suddenly I'm looking at a girl's aquamarine diary.

"What's this?"

"It's your diary when you were nine."

"Oh, my God, I haven't thought of this thing in years. I wrote in it every day for a year." I touch the cover with my fingertip.

"I know. When I saw the blouse, well, look, it matches the diary and the color is so lovely. I read a few entries—"

"You read my diary?" I smile, raise an eyebrow.

"A few weeks ago. I'm sorry—"

"Oh, don't be silly. I don't care. What in the world could be in it? I was only nine. Now, if it were about my college days…"

"Really? I didn't think you were wild in college?"

"We can talk about that later. You know, I saved my allowance to buy it at the drugstore. I remember that. What a cute idea. What's this?" I point to a Post-it note at the back of the book.

She leans closer. "It's the last entry I read before I called and asked you to come home for Christmas."

I turn to the marked page.

December 24

Dear Diary,

This Christmas I want a huge real tree with white lights, pretty ornaments, caroling and big turkey dinner. But most of all for Christmas I want my mother to be home. That would make it perfect.

I stare at the page. I don't remember writing this, but I do remember feeling so lonely on Christmas Day when my mother had to be at the hospital.

Her hand touches my arm. "I didn't realize how you felt and then a few days ago when I read this…"

"I know," I say, gesturing to her watch. "We're both

learning. It wasn't until yesterday that I realized you never had anyone to buy you nice Christmas gifts."

She shakes her head. "But I'm your mother, I should have known. I was so busy trying to make a living for us, be the best doctor for your father, stay away from all my hurtful memories. I forgot about your wishes. I just didn't want you to worry about money the way I had to when I was young."

"Mother, it's okay. We've both made mistakes." I lean over and hug her.

"But the other day, after I read that, I thought, *well, I can't go back, but I can give Gwen her perfect Christmas before it's too late*."

Her last two words make me sit up straighter. "Too late? What do you mean by that? We have so many Christmases in front of us."

She shakes her head, gazes at her watch. "I'm glad we've had this time together. I just wanted this holiday to be perfect for you." She stands, walks over to the tree, touches a branch then comes back to the couch and sits closer to me.

"Something's wrong and you're not telling me," I say.

"I wasn't going to say anything, but I don't want you planning for next year. Not right now."

I stare at her for a moment. "Why not?"

"Because…"

"Mom, tell me!"

"I promised myself I wouldn't tell you until later, until I

found out, because I didn't want to ruin Christmas. But I…I had a test for pancreatic cancer a week ago. I don't have the results yet, but if they aren't good…but then it could be nothing. That's why I wanted this holiday to be everything you wanted." She touches my aquamarine diary I'm still holding.

My heart begins to pound and I feel light-headed. My mother has always been healthy, strong. "Mother…I…do you feel tired? Are you feeling normal?"

"I'm a little tired but I think it's from the worry. My doctor ran some normal yearly tests and saw something odd, so she wanted to check."

"When will you find out?" My heartbeat quickens more.

"The lab promised they'd get the results back tomorrow, early, so I thought we need to celebrate Christmas, then you'd be on your way home and if something came up…"

My diary begins to blur in front of me. Right now nothing matters except finding out my mother is going to be okay.

"I was going to fly home in the morning," I say.

"Yes, I know you have a lot to do. It's important you do that."

"No! I'm not going now. How could I? I'd be so worried. I'll stay, then when you get the good news, we'll celebrate." I gesture to the kitchen. "Maybe the turkey will be thawed out by then."

She laughs. "Gwen, you should go. What about your case?"

"What about your health? Absolutely not. The case will wait. Like you said, I always overprepare anyway." I stand with my diary in my hand. "My mind's made up. I'm going to go call the airline right now and cancel my reservation."

CHAPTER 7

"Janie, come in," I say. She walks through the open door with a big smile on her face. She looks the same, dark hair cut short and her figure trim. She's carrying a shopping bag with presents.

"Hi, honey. How are you? It's been so long." She closes the space between us, puts down her shopping bag and throws her arms around me.

"It's so good to see you," I say, hugging her back.

A moment later we let go and she turns to my mother. "Look who's here. It's good to see you, too, even though it's only been a few days." Janie and my mother hug then break apart.

"Look what Gwen bought me." My mother holds out her arm so Janie can see her new watch. "Isn't it lovely?"

Janie studies the watch then looks at me. "It's beautiful. What a nice gift, Gwen."

"I'm glad she likes it. I challenged the crowds, bought it Christmas Eve."

"Did you put the turkey in?" Janie asks. We both nod at

the same time. "Great." She sniffs the air. "It's starting to smell like Christmas."

My mother smiles, but I think I see the worry hidden in her gaze. "It does, doesn't it? I need to go set the table."

"I'll help, Mom." I head toward the kitchen.

"No, absolutely not." She nods to the Christmas tree. "I want you two to sit by the tree. Visit with Janie, catch up. It won't take me a minute and then I'll join you."

"Please let us help," I say, feeling more worried.

"No! I want to do this by myself." My mother turns and goes into the kitchen.

"Her mind's made up. Might as well let her be," Janie says, touching my shoulder.

"And we both know how that is." I lead her to the couch and we sit close to each other.

"It's so good to see you," she says, patting my hand. "How are you?"

"I'm fine, working too hard as usual, but I'm going to change a little of that."

"It's good you could make time to come home for Christmas. Your mother has missed you since she retired."

I look toward the kitchen then back to Janie. "Did she tell you?"

She nods. "Yes. The other day. That's why she wanted you home. I told her to tell you, but she wouldn't hear of it. She didn't want you to come home only for her health. She wanted you to enjoy Christmas."

"I'm trying," I say, really meaning it. "I changed my flight. Thank goodness she told me. I would have gone home in the morning not knowing. It must be hard for her. She's always been the one taking care of people."

Janie nods. "She'll be fine. She's a strong woman."

"Let's just pray her test comes back negative." I hug her again, then sit back, look at the tree. "We decorated it all by ourselves. Doesn't it look wonderful?"

"It does. I'm proud of you both. I was always so proud of your mother, helping people, saving lives. And I was happy I could be a part of that. Now I'm proud of you. I always have been. You know your mother helped me a lot."

I look at her, turn my head a little. "How is that? It seemed like you were always helping us."

"Most people think that but when she first hired me, I had no skills. I was a young girl who didn't even have a high school education. And I was practically homeless. I was married to an abusive man. Your mother let me stay here until I could get on my feet, get a divorce."

"I never knew that."

"You were just a baby. She worked with me, made sure I went to night school and was always encouraging. I don't know what I would have done without her. She worked hard for a long time. Now I'm glad she has time for herself."

"I just hope the tests..." I stop, unable to finish.

Janie's arm goes around my shoulders. "She'll be fine, honey. I feel it in my bones. And we'll see each other next year, too. We've helped each other. That's the way life is. It's perfect in that way."

"I hope so, Janie. I've never wanted anything more."

December 26

"The lab told you they'd call early this morning?" I ask my mother.

"Yes, Gwen. No matter how many times you ask, the answer is still the same." Mom folds her hands, rests them on the kitchen table.

I try to smile but can't. We've been sitting in the kitchen since 5:00 a.m. I didn't sleep well, and I don't think my mother did, either.

She takes another sip of coffee, places her cup on the napkin in front of her. "We had a good day yesterday, didn't we?"

I nod, force myself to smile. "We did. It was the best. It was so good to see Janie. I didn't realize how much I miss her till yesterday. Thank you for everything. It was so—"

The phone rings and my mother purses her lips. She pushes back her chair and crosses the kitchen, picks up the phone. My heart slams against my ribs. I just wish she would smile so I'd know she's going to be all right.

"Thank you so much," she says, hangs up the phone and looks at me. "They're negative."

With the good news, my heart begins to pound even harder. I stand. "Oh, thank God." I cross the room, hug her hard. Suddenly the kitchen fills with early morning sunlight, as if the day knows my mother is okay.

"Charlene said she wanted to call earlier, but some problems came up. I worked with her for years at the hospital." My mother smiles again then laughs. "Negative is such a wonderful word. Such a beautiful word...perfect. Just a *perfect* word."

I take her hands, dance her around the kitchen, then into the living room where two hours ago I plugged in the Christmas tree lights. I stop, stand very still. "Yes, it's a perfect word." I cross the room to the couch and sit, take a deep breath.

My mother sits next to me. "I'm so happy. The test...all this made me realize how important my relationship with you is. How I want to spend time with you so we can get to know each other better."

I nod. "I didn't want to tell you this before you heard from the lab, but last night I made arrangements to stay here three extra days no matter what news you got. So I don't have to go back until Thursday. I can help you take down the tree, store the decorations and we can talk more."

Her eyes grow wider, misty, and she touches the corners of her eyes. "That's the best present."

"And I have some more news."

"Really?" My mother places her hand on her chest, takes a deep breath. "I appreciate that you're doing this."

I reach over, pat her shoulder, feel more relaxed than I have in days. "Finding out about your test made me realize that life is pretty fragile, and we need to spend more time together. I'd like you to come to Boston in March, for my birthday."

She stares at me for a moment. "That would be wonderful. I'd love to."

"My boss also told me I'm making partner in March so I thought you could come up for a combination birthday-promotion celebration."

"Oh, Gwen, I'm so glad. I'd love to visit. Isn't this a happy day?"

I lean over and hug her again. Then I glance at the tree, get up, go over and pick up my diary and open it to the page that's still marked with a yellow Post-it note. I point to my childish writing.

"I finally got my perfect Christmas, Mother! Today is my perfect Christmas."

Her expression is so relaxed and happy. "I'm glad, Gwen. I'm hoping there will be many more."

"And it just happened. If I hadn't come home, we wouldn't have talked, gotten to know each other better. What more could I ask for?"

"Not much."

I sit on the couch and reach for her hand, hold it gently. "Oh, yes, there is. I want you to promise to go out on a date. That's what I want for my next Christmas present," I say.

She looks surprised. "I'm not sure about that."

I laugh. "I'll make you a deal. I'll go on a date if you will.

Maybe when you come to Boston, we can go to one of those dating services. You know, get a two-for-one discount," I say, then raise an eyebrow.

She laughs and so do I. "Well, I'm not sure about that, either, but I'll try to have a date by next Christmas if I get up enough nerve."

I lean over and hug her again. "Merry Christmas, Mother. Merry, merry Christmas."

* * * * *

Experience entertaining women's fiction for every woman who has wondered "what's next?" in her life.

Turn the page for a sneak preview of a new book from Harlequin NEXT,

WHY IS MURDER ON THE MENU, ANYWAY?

by Stevi Mittman

On sale December 26, wherever books are sold.

Design Tip of the Day

> Ambience is everything. Imagine eating a foie gras at a luncheonette counter or a side of coleslaw at Le Cirque. It's not a matter of food but one of atmosphere. Remember that when planning your dining room design.
>
> —Tips from *Teddi.com*

"Now that's the kind of man you should be looking for," my mother, the self-appointed keeper of my shelf-life stamp, says. She points with her fork at a man in the corner of the Steak-Out Restaurant, a dive I've just been hired to redecorate. Making this restaurant look four-star will be hard, but not half as hard as getting through lunch without strangling the woman across the table from me. "*He* would make a good husband."

"Oh, you can tell that from across the room?" I ask, wondering how it is she can forget that when we had trouble getting rid of my last husband, she shot him. "Besides being ten minutes away from death if he actually eats all that steak, he's twenty years too old for me and—shallow woman that I am—twenty pounds too heavy. Besides, I am *so* not looking for another husband here. I'm looking to design a new image for this place, looking for some sense of ambience, some feeling, something I can build a proposal on for them."

My mother studies the man in the corner, tilting her head, the better to gauge his age, I suppose. I think she's grimacing, but with all the Botox and Restylane injected into that face, it's hard to tell. She takes another bite of her steak, chews slowly so that I don't miss the fact that the steak is a poor cut and tougher than it should be. "You're concentrating on the wrong kind of proposal," she says finally. "Just look at this place, Teddi. It's a dive. There are hardly any other diners. What does *that* tell you about the food?"

"That they cater to a dinner crowd and it's lunchtime," I tell her.

I don't know what I was thinking bringing her here with me. I suppose I thought it would be better than eating alone. There really are days when my common sense goes on vacation. Clearly, this is one of them. I mean, really, did I not resolve just a few months ago that I would not let my mother get to me anymore?

What good are New Year's resolutions, anyway?

Mario approaches the man's table and my mother studies him while they converse. Eventually Mario leaves the table with a huff, after which the diner glances up and meets my mother's gaze. I think she's smiling at him. That or she's got indigestion. They size each other up.

I concentrate on making sketches in my notebook and try to ignore the fact that my mother is flirting. At nearly seventy, she's developed an unhealthy interest in members of the opposite sex to whom she isn't married.

According to my father, who has broken the TMI rule and given me Too Much Information, she has no interest in sex with him. Better, I suppose, to be clued in on what they aren't doing in the bedroom than have to hear what they might be doing.

"He's not so old," my mother says, noticing that I have barely touched the Chinese chicken salad she warned me not to get. "He's got about as many years on you as you have on your little cop friend."

She does this to make me crazy. I know it, but it works all the same. "Drew Scoones is not my little 'friend.' He's a detective with whom I—"

"Screwed around," my mother says. I must look shocked, because my mother laughs at me and asks if I think she doesn't know the "lingo."

What I thought she didn't know was that Drew and I actually tangled in the sheets. And, since it's possible she's just fishing, I sidestep the issue and tell her that Drew is just a couple of years younger than me and that I don't need reminding. I dig into my salad with renewed vigor, determined to show my mother that Chinese chicken salad in a steak place was not the stupid choice it's proving to be.

After a few more minutes of my picking at the wilted leaves on my plate, the man my mother has me nearly engaged to pays his bill and heads past us toward the back of the restaurant. I watch my mother take in his shoes, his suit and the diamond pinkie ring that seems to be cutting off the circulation in his little finger.

"Such nice hands," she says after the man is out of sight. "Manicured." She and I both stare at my hands. I have two popped acrylics that are being held on at weird angles by bandages. My cuticles are ragged and there's marker decorating my right hand from measuring carelessly when I did a drawing for a customer.

Twenty minutes later she's disappointed that he managed to leave the restaurant without our noticing. He will join the list of the ones I let get away. I will hear about him twenty years from now when—according to my mother—my children will be grown and I will still be single, living pathetically alone with several dogs and cats.

After my ex, that sounds good to me.

The waitress tells us that our meal has been taken care of by the management and, after thanking Mario, the owner, complimenting him on the wonderful meal and assuring him that once I have redecorated his place people will be flocking here in droves (I actually use those words and ignore my mother when she rolls her eyes), my mother and I head for the restroom.

My father—unfortunately not with us today—has the

patience of a saint. He got it over the years of living with my mother. She, perhaps as a result, figures he has the patience for both of them, and feels justified having none. For her, no rules apply, and a little thing like a picture of a man on the door to a public restroom is certainly no barrier to using the john. In all fairness, it does seem silly to stand and wait for the ladies' room if no one is using the men's room.

Still, it's the idea that rules don't apply to her, signs don't apply to her, conventions don't apply to her. She knocks on the door to the men's room. When no one answers she gestures to me to go in ahead. I tell her that I can certainly wait for the ladies' room to be free and she shrugs and goes in herself.

Not a minute later there is a bloodcurdling scream from behind the men's room door.

"Mom!" I yell. "Are you all right?"

Mario comes running over, the waitress on his heels. Two customers head our way while my mother continues to scream.

I try the door, but it is locked. I yell for her to open it and she fumbles with the knob. When she finally manages to unlock and open it, she is white behind her two streaks of blush, but she is on her feet and appears shaken but not stirred.

"What happened?" I ask her. So do Mario and the waitress and the few customers who have migrated to the back of the place.

She points toward the bathroom and I go in, thinking it serves her right for using the men's room. But I see nothing amiss.

She gestures toward the stall, and, like any self-respecting and suspicious woman, I poke the door open with one finger, expecting the worst.

What I find is worse than the worst.

The husband my mother picked out for me is sitting on the toilet. His pants are puddled around his ankles, his hands are hanging at his sides. Pinned to his chest is some sort of Health Department certificate.

Oh, and there is a large, round, bloodless bullet hole between his eyes.

Four Nassau County police officers are securing the area, waiting for the detectives and crime scene personnel to show up. They are trying, though not very hard, to comfort my mother, who in another era would be considered to be suffering from the vapors. Less tactful in the twenty-first century, I'd say she was losing it. That is, if I didn't know her better, know she was milking it for everything it was worth.

My mother loves attention. As it begins to flag, she swoons and claims to feel faint. Despite four No Smoking signs, my mother insists it's all right for her to light up because, after all, she's in shock. Not to mention that signs, as we know, don't apply to her.

When asked not to smoke, she collapses mournfully in a chair and lets her head loll to the side, all without mussing her hair.

Eventually, the detectives show up to find the four patrolmen all circled around her, debating whether to administer CPR, smelling salts or simply call the paramedics. I, however, know just what will snap her to attention.

"Detective Scoones," I say loudly. My mother parts the sea of cops.

"We have to stop meeting like this," he says lightly to me, but I can feel him checking me over with his eyes, making sure I'm all right while pretending not to care.

"What have you got in those pants?" my mother asks him, coming to her feet and staring at his crotch accusingly. "*Baydar?* Everywhere we Bayers are, you turn up. You don't expect me to buy that this is a coincidence, I hope."

Drew tells my mother that it's nice to see her, too, and asks if it's his fault that her daughter seems to attract disasters.

Charming to be made to feel like the bearer of a plague.

He asks how I am.

"Just peachy," I tell him. "I seem to be making a habit of finding dead bodies, my mother is driving me crazy and the catering hall I booked two freakin' years ago for Dana's bat mitzvah has just been shut down by the Board of Health!"

"Glad to see your luck's finally changing," he says, giving me a quick squeeze around the shoulders before turning his attention to the patrolmen, asking what they've got, whether they've taken any statements, moved anything, all the sort of stuff you see on TV, without any of the drama. That is, if you don't count my mother's threats to faint every few minutes when she senses no one's paying attention to her.

Mario tells his waitstaff to bring everyone espresso, which I decline because I'm wired enough. Drew pulls him aside and a minute later I'm handed a cup of coffee that smells divinely of Kahlúa.

The man knows me well. Too well.

His partner, whom I've met once or twice, says he'll interview the kitchen staff. Drew asks Mario if he minds if he takes statements from the patrons first and gets to him and the wait staff afterward.

"No, no," Mario tells him. "Do the patrons first." Drew raises his eyebrow at me like he wants to know if I get the double entendre. I try to look bored.

"What is it with you and murder victims?" he asks me when we sit down at a table in the corner.

I search them out so that I can see you again, I almost say, but I'm afraid it will sound desperate instead of sarcastic.

My mother, lighting up and daring him with a look to tell her not to, reminds him that *she* was the one to find the body.

Drew asks what happened *this time*. My mother tells him how the man in the john was "taken" with me, couldn't take his eyes off me and blatantly flirted with both of us. To his credit, Drew doesn't laugh, but his smirk is undeniable to the trained eye. And I've had my eye trained on him for nearly a year now.

"While he was noticing you," he asks me, "did *you* notice anything about him? Was he waiting for anyone? Watching for anything?"

I tell him that he didn't appear to be waiting or watching. That he made no phone calls, was fairly intent on eating and did, indeed, flirt with my mother. This last bit Drew takes with a grain of salt, which was the way it was intended.

"And he had a short conversation with Mario," I tell him. "I think he might have been unhappy with the food, though he didn't send it back."

Drew asks what makes me think he was dissatisfied, and I tell him that the discussion seemed acrimonious and that Mario looked distressed when he left the table. Drew makes a note and says he'll look into it and asks about anyone else in the restaurant. Did I see anyone who didn't seem to belong, anyone who was watching the victim, anyone looking suspicious?

"Besides my mother?" I ask him, and Mom huffs and blows her cigarette smoke in my direction.

I tell him that there were several deliveries, the kitchen staff going in and out the back door to grab a smoke. He stops me and asks what I was doing checking out the back door of the restaurant.

Proudly—because, while he was off forgetting me, dropping by only once in a while to say hi to Jesse, my son, or drop something by for one of my daughters that he thought they might like, I was getting on with my life—I tell him that I'm decorating the place.

He looks genuinely impressed. "Commercial customers?

That's great," he says. Okay, that's what he *ought* to say. What he actually says is "Whatever pays the bills."

"Howard Rosen, the famous restaurant critic, got her the job," my mother says. "You met him—the good-looking, distinguished gentleman with the *real* job, something to be proud of. I guess you've never read his reviews in *Newsday*."

Drew, without missing a beat, tells her that Howard's reviews are on the top of his list, as soon as he learns how to read.

"I only meant—" my mother starts, but both of us assure her that we know just what she meant.

"So," Drew says. "Deliveries?"

I tell him that Mario would know better than I, but that I saw vegetables come in, maybe fish and linens.

"This is the second restaurant job Howard's got her," my mother tells Drew.

"At least she's getting *something* out of the relationship," he says.

"If he were here," my mother says, ignoring the insinuation, "he'd be comforting her instead of interrogating her. He'd be making sure we're both all right after such an ordeal."

"I'm sure he would," Drew agrees, then looks me in the eyes as if he's measuring my tolerance for shock. Quietly he adds, "But then maybe he doesn't know just what strong stuff your daughter's made of."

It's the closest thing to a tender moment I can expect from Drew Scoones. My mother breaks the spell. "She gets that from me," she says.

Both Drew and I take a minute, probably to pray that's all I inherited from her.

"I'm just trying to save you some time and effort," my mother tells him. "My money's on Howard."

Drew withers her with a look and mutters something that sounds suspiciously like "fool's gold." Then he excuses himself to go back to work.

I catch his sleeve and ask if it's all right for us to leave. He says sure, he knows where we live. I say goodbye to Mario. I assure him that I will have some sketches for him in a few days, all the while hoping that this murder doesn't cancel his redecorating plans. I need the money desperately, the alternative being borrowing from my parents and being strangled by the strings.

My mother is strangely quiet all the way to her house. She doesn't tell me what a loser Drew Scoones is—despite his good looks—and how I was obviously drooling over him. She doesn't ask me where Howard is taking me tonight or warn me not to tell my father about what happened because he will worry about us both and no doubt insist we see our respective psychiatrists.

She fidgets nervously, opening and closing her purse over and over again.

"You okay?" I ask her. After all, she's just found a dead man on the toilet, and tough as she is that's got to be upsetting.

When she doesn't answer me I pull over to the side of the road.

"Mom?" She refuses to meet my eyes. "You want me to take you to see Dr. Cohen?"

She looks out the window as if she's just realized we're on Broadway in Woodmere. "Aren't we near Marvin's Jewelers?" she asks, pulling something out of her purse.

"What have you got, Mother?" I ask, prying open her fingers to find the murdered man's ring.

"It was on the sink," she says in answer to my dropped jaw. "I was going to get his name and address and have you return it to him so that he could ask you out. I thought it was a sign that the two of you were meant to be together."

"He's dead, Mom. You understand that, right?" I ask. You never can tell when my mother is fine and when she's in la-la land.

"Well, I didn't know that," she shouts at me. "Not at the time."

I ask why she didn't give it to Drew, realize that she wouldn't give Drew the time in a clock shop and add, "…or one of the other policemen?"

"For heaven's sake," she tells me. "The man is dead, Teddi, and I took his ring. How would that look?"

Before I can tell her it looks just the way it is, she pulls out a cigarette and threatens to light it.

"I mean, really," she says, shaking her head like it's my brains that are loose. "What does he need with it now?"